I0608198

THE
PORTRAIT

AND OTHER TALES OF HORROR AND HUMOR

HAROLD (HP) PHIPPS

Copyright © 2022 by Harold (HP) Phipps

All rights reserved. This book may not be reproduced or stored in whole or in part by any means without the written permission of the author except for brief quotations for the purpose of review.

ISBN: 978-1-954614-88-8

Phipps. Harold (HP)
The Portrait.
Edited by: Melissa Long

Warren publishing

Published by Warren Publishing
Charlotte, NC
www.warrenpublishing.net
Printed in the United States

Table of Contents

THE WATER LADY

Often after services at the Healing Waters Baptist Church, my grandparents, Morgan and Trula Grayson, would eat Sunday dinner with family or friends from the church. Neither of my grandparents had a driver's license, so they depended on neighbors and kinfolk to transport them to and from the church. My grandmother had three brothers, Scott, Al, and Bill Blevins. As a boy and backseat passenger, I traveled many winding gravel roads for Sunday dinners at my uncles' farms in the Crumpler, Chestnut Hill, and Grassy Creek communities in the North Carolina mountain county of Ashe. I had many satisfying Sunday dinners at their homes—fried chicken, mashed potatoes, creamed corn, sweet potato casseroles, green beans cooked with fatback, yeast rolls or buttered biscuits, and sweet tea. Desserts included pies, cakes, and banana puddings. Occasionally, the fried chicken was replaced by country ham.

It was on one of these trips that I first heard of a ghost known as the Water Lady.

Around a sharp curve in the road, I saw a tall, rock chimney like a lofty tombstone standing alone. Not a vestige remained of the house it had warmed. Nearby, a creek, wide with swift water, pushed its way over and around rocks and boulders. The chimney, made of heavy stones carefully placed and constructed without a sign of brick masonry, sparked my grandmother's memory, or at least kindled her imagination.

"That chimney was once part of the Edwards house," she said. "The family is gone now; they've been gone for years. The house is gone, too, washed away by the big flood in 1940. The 'forty flood took away the family's mill and millstone too. The house was once haunted by the Water Lady's spirit."

"The Water Lady?" I asked. "Tell me about her."

"Not now," said my grandmother. "A movin' automobile ain't the right place to tell a ghost story. Slow this car down, Al. I'm fixin' to get car sick. We'll be at Al's place soon, Hal. There will be a fire goin' in the fireplace. That'll be the perfect place to tell a ghost story."

"Trula, don't fill the boy's head with your scary stories," my grandfather said. "You know he had trouble sleeping last week after watching *The Twilight Zone*." My grandfather turned to me and said, "Hal, I don't believe in ghosts. I want you to know that."

"I don't believe in ghosts either, Grandpa, but I like ghost stories. I want to hear about the Water Lady."

"Morgan, you heard the boy. He wants to hear a ghost story, and I want to tell him one."

"Suit yourselves," said my grandfather. He sighed and shifted his shoulders, assuming a more comfortable position in the automobile's front passenger seat. He stared silently at the road ahead of us. He knew that both my grandmother and I had a stubborn streak and that the Water Lady's ghost story would be told sooner or later.

* * *

My grandmother and I were seated in front of Uncle Al's cozy fireplace when she began the tale of the Water Lady, who had haunted the missing Edwards house. However, the story was interrupted by the dinner preparations. "Trula, come help with the biscuits. You can finish your ghost story later," called a voice from the kitchen. The voice belonged to Aunt Della, Uncle Al's wife, who made the best banana pudding I had ever tasted.

Following the dinner, I managed to piece together the Water Lady's story by asking my grandmother, the chief storyteller in our family, and the other adults questions about the female phantom and the place she had haunted. My grandfather described a working mill like the one Clinton Edwards operated and told me how the flowing creek water powered the waterwheel, which was used to move the heavy millstone and, thereby, grind grain into flour. My uncle told me how the old rock chimneys and fireplaces were constructed by hand and why they often lasted much longer than the dwellings they warmed.

My grandmother and my aunt spoke of Olivia Edwards's death and the subsequent hauntings. I learned that Aunt Della, who was just a little girl at the time, had attended Olivia Edwards's funeral. "The casket was kept closed," she said. "I suppose her face was disfigured because of the way she died."

That was when my grandmother chimed in again and told my eleven-year-old self the story of the Water Lady. Her voice was strong and clear, and the other adults remained silent during the storytelling. Uncle Al's old Chihuahua, Buddy, jumped up into his lap and promptly fell asleep. I leaned forward in my chair so I wouldn't miss a single word. I wanted to hear all about the Water Lady so I could tell her ghost story one day.

***

When my grandparents were children, there was a large, white house attached to the rock chimney, and a family of five lived there. A busy mill on the property supplemented the family's farm income. The rushing creek had been dammed, creating a pond and providing water power to work the mill, which had been in the Edwards family for several generations. From Ashe County farms nearby and far away, farmers brought their wagon loads of grain to be ground into cornmeal or wheat flour by the miller. Farmers' teenaged sons had another reason to come to the mill: the miller's beautiful daughter, Olivia Edwards.

Only seventeen, Olivia Edwards had long raven-black hair, bright blue eyes, and pale skin. She preferred to dress in white and was seldom seen wearing any other color. When outside, she carried a white parasol to shade her face and eyes. Olivia Edwards had an unusual aversion to the sun. Direct sunlight produced freckles on her fair skin, and she thought the skin speckles made her less attractive.

The miller, Clinton Edwards, was proud of his daughter's beauty and character. She sang in her Baptist church's choir, was an A student in her one-room school, and visited the sick in her community, often preparing meals for them. Her father's pride in Olivia was equaled only by her mother's. Mrs. Edwards had instructed her daughter in the art of sewing. Together, she and Olivia had begun making quilts to sell and to give as gifts. One of Olivia's quilts had even earned first place at the county fair.

***

Young Olivia was engaged to be married on the Sunday before Christmas day. The mere mention of her fiancé's name, Brian Hunter, would brighten her eyes and bring a smile to her face. Brian was Dundee Hunter's only son and had assumed most of the duties involved in running the Hunter farm, which included many acres of bottomlands along the New River. Brian was tall and lean with dark, curly hair and clear blue eyes. He and Olivia had begun their courtship when she was only fifteen and Brian was a lad of sixteen. They had met at school, and their courtship included church socials, sleigh rides, and picnics on the banks of the New River. Olivia was just seventeen when she accepted Brian's proposal of marriage.

"Oh, I hope we don't have a deep snow on my wedding day. I don't think I could bear it," she had said.

The day after Thanksgiving, she would turn eighteen and be of marrying age.

However, the miller's daughter never reached her eighteenth birthday. During the summer, she came down with a sickness known only to doctors of those early days as "the fever." The local doctor, who had arrived on horseback, said there was nothing to do but put the young girl to bed in her bedroom on the second level of the house. "Keep fresh water in her bedroom. Give it to her when she thirsts," he said. "I shall pray for your daughter, Mrs. Edwards. I can do little else."

Olivia's mother sat by her daughter's bedside night and day. Using cloths cooled by spring water, Mary Edwards bathed her daughter's fevered brow. On the second day, the girl became delirious. She thrashed about on her bed and cried out for water. "I thirst! I thirst! Bring more water!" she wailed. On the third day of the fever, she descended into a deep coma. Gathered at the bedside, the family prayed for her recovery. Outside, a summer rain storm buffeted the house's roof. Wind and rain rushed through the bedroom's open window until the miller rose and slammed it shut. The bedridden girl groaned and shifted her position, but she did not awaken.

At midnight on the third night of her illness, Olivia Edwards sat upright in bed. Her mother, exhausted, slept soundly in a chair beside the bed. The girl, clothed only in her white nightgown, rose from the bed and walked out of the room. She silently made her way down the stairs. The somnambulist paused in the kitchen long enough to grasp a white bonnet hanging by the door, and place it on her head. Then she went outside into the cool, black night.

The dew-moistened grass gave her some relief from the fever as she, with her eyes half closed and heavy-lidded, made her way to the millpond. Froglets chirped from the pond. A water snake slithered soundlessly into the water as Olivia reached the edge of the pond. After a few steps, she was up to her knees in the murky water. The cooling water against her skin urged her forward. Soon the pond water was up to her armpits, yet still she walked on. Her head slipped beneath the millpond's surface, and she drowned without a struggle.

The next morning, the miller's wife awakened and discovered her daughter missing. The family searched the house and grounds for her. It was her younger brother who, peering through an upstairs window, caught sight of the white bonnet floating on the pond's still water. It was her older brother who, after several deep dives, brought his sister's body to the surface. Her corpse was discolored, having taken on a bluish hue. Her hands and feet were wrinkled, but her face retained its beauty for hours after her body was recovered. Then her face began to deteriorate with deep lines forming around her mouth and nose and eyes.

Within a few days, she was buried in a cemetery less than half a mile from the pond that took her life. Her casket remained closed during the memorial service. The minister's words provided little comfort. In their pew, Olivia's family wept as they stared fixedly at the church's floor. At her burial, her young fiancé was inconsolable. To his family, he had spoken of nightmares.

In his dreams, he saw Olivia sitting on large stones at the bottom of the deep pond with her long, dark hair floating about her head. Her face was turned upward, and she seemed to be reaching for the pond's surface. His parents watched him closely for many days, for Brian Hunter had threatened suicide. Shotguns and rifles belonging to Brian and his father were locked away.

After a year had passed, Clinton Edwards sold the mill, the house, and the surrounding property. He took his wife and sons to Virginia to start a new life. His neighbors said that too many memories and too many bad dreams had driven the miller and his family away.

The hauntings began when a new family occupied the miller's house. The newcomers, the Johnson family, often awoke to find the downstairs furniture had been rearranged during the night, always with the largest chair pulled close to the stone fireplace. Upon close examination, it was found that the chair's upholstery was soaked with water, and the rugs in front of the fireplace were drenched.

One bedroom upstairs, Olivia's former bedroom, was always dank and depressive no matter how bright and warm the day outside. A black mold, not easily removed, clung to all the bedroom's walls. Condensation formed on the inside of the windowpanes making it difficult to see the sturdy oak tree outside. Sometimes, from inside the wall opposite the single window in the small bedroom, the Johnsons heard muffled gasping, hissing, and coughing sounds. The sounds were indistinct and attributed to bats or mice crawling within the walls.

Once, a child in the household, returning from fetching himself a dipper of cool water from the kitchen downstairs, knocked on his parents' bedroom door and asked, "Who is the lady in the kitchen, Mommy?"

"There's no one in the kitchen, Joey."

"Yes, there is."

He told of meeting a pale young woman dressed in white and soaked to the skin, with tangled curls of long, black hair. "She asked me if I wanted to walk with her down to the pond. She begged me to go. She's lonely. I told her Daddy wouldn't let me go down there after dark. She stutters when she talks, like Uncle James. She's a nice lady, though. I could tell."

The boy's family sold the house shortly after the occurrence.

The house, the mill, and the surrounding farmland had many owners in the following years. None stayed for very long. The property sold for less and less as the years passed, and gradually the house and its outbuildings fell into disrepair.

Over the years, the girl-phantom was seen many times, albeit always at night. She was never an evil specter, and after their initial jolt of adrenaline, the flesh-and-blood observers of the Water Lady felt a disquieting sadness and solemn pity for the dripping apparition. There were reports of the ghost opening her mouth and moving her gray lips and black tongue—water trickling from her lower lip and chin—as if she were trying to speak, but no understandable words came forth. She could only make strange, guttural sounds.

Because of the hauntings, the property became virtually worthless. The last owner was from the city of Pittsburgh, Pennsylvania, a man who had little patience with mountain people or their made-up ghosts. Having bought the property at a bargain price, he began repairing the house himself, transforming the structure into his vision of the perfect summer home.

From a shed behind the house, he carried logs and kindling to the house's rock fireplace. He built a fire and confirmed that the flue was working properly. The Pennsylvanian decided to start a fire every evening to ward off the night's chill, for he had discovered that in the North Carolina mountains, a warm midsummer day could be followed by a cold summer night.

Late one night, after having spent most of the day tearing out the half-rotten planks of the front porch, the new owner retired to a bedroom upstairs where he spread woolen blankets on the floor. He threw a stained white sheet over the blankets. The room was lit by flickering candles. He folded his shirt to use as a pillow and lay down. As was his custom, he smoked his pipe for a few minutes before he placed it, along with his tobacco and matches, on a small wooden box that served as a makeshift table. He extinguished the two candles stationed on the box. He then turned on his side, closed his eyes, and tried to sleep.

Outside, a feeble summer storm was brewing, and flashes of lightning, unaccompanied by thunder, illuminated the bedroom. The man could not sleep. A feeling of oppression and gloom filled him almost to the point of nausea. He turned and reached for the box upon which rested his pipe, tobacco, and matches. Instead of touching the familiar objects in the darkness, his hand felt rough skin and matted, wet hair. A lightning flash revealed to him a strange young woman in white clothing, kneeling next to him. She stared at him with questioning blue eyes. A long, reptilian tongue darted from between her wet lips. Then she opened her mouth, wider than the witness thought possible. Her sharp teeth were covered with green pond scum, and water poured from her gaping jaws. The bedroom darkened. Then lightning flashed again, accompanied by thunder as the storm intensified. For an instant, the room brightened as if it were noon instead of midnight.

The eerie girl was gone.

The wooden floor was soaked.

The man stood up, his legs shaking, and lurched forward in pitch blackness. He made his way toward the stairwell. A lightning bolt struck near the house, splitting the oak tree just outside the bedroom window. Briefly, he was surrounded by light and sound. In a puddle near the stairs, he saw a tiny minnow flipping and flicking, seeking, in vain, deeper water. Then darkness flooded the stairwell once more.

Feeling his way in the darkness, the man made his way, step-by-step, downstairs. The dread of meeting *her* on the stairway stiffened his back. He stumbled once but maintained his downward pace. A strange sound halted him until he realized it was the chattering of his teeth.

At last downstairs, the property owner, aided by the light from the dying flames and fading embers in the fireplace, found matches and lit a coal oil lamp. He wrapped himself in blankets and spent the rest of the night sitting in the lamplight next to a roaring fireplace into which he fed chunks of rotten wood fetched from the decaying steps of the front porch. He shivered and moved closer to the fire. The intense flames and falling embers could not warm him. He left the next day and never returned.

The house and mill are gone now. Lush summer grasses sprinkled with dandelions conceal what once was the pond. Just the rock chimney remains, and it is covered by vines and surrounded by briars. Nearby, the winding gravel road of my youth has been paved. The wide, rushing creek endures and has become a fisherman's paradise, yielding bass and trout. Years have passed, and no one has reported seeing the ghost my grandmother called the Water Lady.

May her spirit find rest, and may God have mercy on her innocent soul.

THE OPAL WINIFRED SPECIAL:
INTERVIEWING THE VENOMOUS SNAKES OF NORTH CAROLINA

OPAL WINIFRED: Welcome to our show this afternoon! Today, we're coming to you live from the Schaefer Center for the Performing Arts on the campus of Appalachian State University in Boone, North Carolina. We have four special guests today representing the four types of venomous snakes found in North Carolina: Mister Timber Rattlesnake, Mister Coral Snake, Mister Copperhead, and Mister Cottonmouth. We hope to educate our television audience about venomous snakes and dispel some of the myths about them. Let us begin with Mister Timber Rattlesnake. Mister Timber Rattlesnake, I understand you are representing several types of rattlesnakes found in North Carolina.

TIMBER: Howdy, Oprie, an' howdy to you'uns out in Tellyvision Land. Yore right as rain, Oprie. I represent several rattlin' snakes, all found in the Tar Heel State. I represent the timber rattler, the canebrake rattler, a little feller from eastern North Carolina called "the pygmy rattler," and another down-easter, the big daddy of all us rattlers, the eastern diamondback. Did ye know that one of them critters reached ninety-six inches in length? Woowee! Now thars a snake what is a snake! Heh! Heh! Heh!

CORAL: Excuse me, Miss Winifred, but before this laughing country bumpkin goes any further, I feel I must clear something up. Some herpetologists believe that the canebrake rattlesnake, with its sandy, pink scales, is just a color variation of the timber rattlesnake. I've seen many canebrake rattlesnakes, and after seeing Mister Timber Rattlesnake, I tend to agree with those scientists.

TIMBER: I'll not dispute bein' close kin to a canebrake rattler, but I don't like yore highfalutin manners, Mister Coral Snake. Ye set thar with them purty black, yeller, and red rings wrapped around yore body an' think yore better'n the rest of us. But ye ain't. Why, look at yore head! There ain't no pit! I'll bet yore not even a pit viper like me an' Mister Cottonmouth an' Mister Copperhead.

CORAL: You are correct! Coral snakes certainly aren't pit vipers. I am, thank goodness, very different from the three of you. You three are very similar. I am dissimilar, not only in the beauty of my colorful skin, but also in many other ways. I am unique, and, Mister Timber Rattlesnake, I am your superior in all ways.

OPAL WINIFRED: Let's learn more about pit vipers, and later, Mister Coral Snake will have an opportunity to tell us about coral snakes. Would you begin, Mister Cottonmouth? By the way, Mister Timber Rattlesnake, would you please stop making that terrible whirring sound?

TIMBER: I'll try, Miss Oprie, but that dadgum coral snake has got me all riled up. When I git this way, mah tail jest natcherly starts twitchin'. I'll try to control it so Cottonmouth can tell ever'body all about us pit vipers. That sissified coral snake better keep his dang mouth shet.

COTTONMOUTH: Miss Winifred, if you look closely, you will notice that my and Copperhead's tails are vibrating rapidly. We react this way when we are angered or threatened. In dry leaves, Copperhead and I sound very much like a rattlesnake. Mister Coral Snake has irritated and offended the three of us by suggesting that pit vipers are inferior in some way to the coral snake. Pit vipers, Miss Winifred, are considered by most herpetologists to be the most highly developed of all serpents.

TIMBER: Hot dang! Go on an' tell it, Cottonmouth! Ye shore talk purty and not one bit uppity.

COTTONMOUTH: Thank you, Timber. Miss Winifred, the pit located just beneath each nostril of a pit viper is a heat-sensing receptor which allows us to zero in on the body heat of our prey. Once our prey is located, we strike with a powerful, frontward thrust. Our retractable fangs are fully forward, and our heads move with terrific speed. Long, hypodermic-like fangs inject venom into our prey. The venom, a cocktail of toxins but primarily a hemotoxic poison, breaks down the cells of the victim. Internal hemorrhaging occurs, followed by cardiovascular shock along with kidney and respiratory failure.

TIMBER: Jest talkin' 'bout it makes me hongry! Mice and chipmunks is mah fav'rites. Deelicious! Miss Oprie, y'all wouldn't have a rat or hamster 'round here, woodjee? I ain't et no prey in months. But that ain't nuthin'. Snakes can survive over a year without no food, but it just ain't normal nor natchral. Us timber rattlers may eat as many as twenty meals a year or as few as six. Hey, Copperhead, ye ain't said nary a word. Cat got yore forked tongue? Can't ye tell us 'bout what ye eat?

COPPERHEAD: My principal food is little gray mice. Small birds, frogs, and insects are also nice. But there's something special that brings the copperhead fame. I am known by many wonderful names—"chunkhead," "highland moccasin," and "adder" to name a few. Some humans call me the "house pilot" too.

TIMBER: Well, ain't that a purty way of talkin'?

CORAL: Ye gads! Must I be surrounded by pit vipers and subjected to a hillbilly ignoramus who calls himself "a timber rattlesnake," and a copperhead who spews forth drivel in a vain attempt at poetry? Really, Miss Winifred! When may I have my turn to relate the glories of the coral snake?

OPAL WINIFRED: You will get your turn, Mister Coral Snake, but I find this discussion of prey fascinating. Mister Cottonmouth, what creatures do you eat?

COTTONMOUTH: My favorites are fish, frogs, salamanders, other snakes, lizards, baby turtles, birds, and small mammals. I once ate a baby alligator, but it gave me indigestion.

TIMBER: Ye know a baby skunk'll do me the exack same way. I et one one time, an' I like to have puked. But a rabbit or a squirrel jest the right size, now that's good eatin'. By the way, Miss Oprie, have ye seen any mice 'round this buildin' or maybe under it? I'm powerful hongry.

OPAL WINIFRED: No, I haven't, Timber. Perhaps after the show, you can go investigate. But right now, I have another question for Mister Cottonmouth. Why do they call you "Cottonmouth"?

COTTONMOUTH: Cottonmouths are semi-aquatic serpents, sometimes called "water moccasins." We sometimes stand our ground when approached. If we feel threatened, we will throw our heads backward and open our mouths wide, revealing a white interior—hence the name "cottonmouth." The coppery-red head of my smaller friend explains his name, and we all know why rattlesnakes are called "rattlesnakes."

COPPERHEAD: Pit vipers are great whether old or young. Tell Opal about our fantastic tongues.

COTTONMOUTH: All snakes have wonderful tongues, Copperhead, not just pit vipers. Every snake's tongue is forked and protrudes for several seconds each time it is flicked through a notch in the upper jaw. When a snake's tongue is back inside its mouth, the tongue transfers collected molecules to the roof of the reptile's mouth. An opening there leads to a structure known as Jacobson's organ. The sensitive cells of Jacobson's organ help the snake identify the molecules and source from which they came. Young timber rattlesnakes can reach their winter den by using Jacobson's organ to find and follow a trail left by an adult rattler.

TIMBER: Baby timber rattlers with their little, button tails! Cutest things ye ever did see! Mah mate birthed five babies last September. Nary one of 'em was over twelve or thirteen inches long. Purty little snakes, they was. Nothin' warms my cold-blooded heart faster'n seein' a little, baby rattlesnake all coiled up an' ready to strike.

COTTONMOUTH: Speaking of baby snakes, Timber, we should inform Opal and our television audience that female pit vipers are viviparous, which means they give birth to live young. Birthing usually takes place in August or September. Snakes such as the coral snake are oviparous, which means they produce eggs that hatch after leaving the body. Coral snake eggs are very elongated and hatch in August or September after an incubation period of seventy to ninety days. Newly hatched coral snakes are about seven inches long.

CORAL: My word, Cottonmouth, you are well-informed. Your knowledge surprises me, especially your knowledge of my species, the beautiful coral snake. Miss Winifred, is it my turn to give you information on my species?

OPAL WINIFRED: Wait just a few more minutes, Mister Coral Snake. First, I'd like to know more about serpent coloration. Could you four tell us something about your interesting colors and markings? All of you are beautiful in your own way.

TIMBER: Aw shucks! Miss Oprie, yore sweeter'n a fat rabbit in a strawberry patch in early June. We are all right purty snakes, ain't we?

COPPERHEAD: Light and shadows shift and change like seasons. Our colors and markings all have reasons. Coral's colors give a warning to stay away. My color conceals me from predator and prey.

COTTONMOUTH: We pit vipers have camouflage that is called "disruptive coloration." Our markings take the form of blotching, saddles, or zigzag shapes along our entire lengths. Mister Copperhead provides an excellent example of light and dark brown disruptive markings that render him almost invisible on the leafy forest floor. Likewise, Timber is perfectly camouflaged in his rocky, mountainous terrain, and I can lie unnoticed, blending in with the soil and vegetation in my swampy home. In contrast, Mister Coral Snake, with his bright red, yellow, and black colors, warns predators that he is dangerous. This is called "warning coloration." Coral snakes in the United States have the bright red rings bordered by yellow rings. Some harmless snakes protect themselves by adapting the same bright colors of the coral snake, but the red rings on harmless snakes are bordered by black. Copperhead, do you have a poem that might prove helpful if a human encounters a brightly colored snake?

COPPERHEAD: Red on black, venom lack. Red on yellow, kill a fellow.

OPAL: Useful information, Copperhead. But now, let's turn to another question. I know that all snakes are carnivorous, and I know that snakes are ectotherms—creatures that cannot produce their own body heat as opposed to endotherms such as mammals and birds. Here's what I don't know: What dangers do you face in the wild? What types of animals prey on you fellows?

COTTONMOUTH: We are most vulnerable, of course, when we are very young. I'll name a few creatures that prey on the four of us: raccoons, other snakes, bobcats, foxes, alligators, opossums, dogs, cats, predatory birds such as red-tailed hawks—

TIMBER: Red-tailed hawks! Ye coulda talked all day an' not mentioned them varmints. One like to have kilt me when I was a little feller. I was restin' on a rocky ledge in the warm sunshine of mah first summer, and here comes the big bird swoopin' down on me—all fury an' feathers an' beak an' talons! The bird's talons scraped the rocks an' one tore into mah side. Looky here, Oprie, ye kin still see the scar. I slid into a crevice quick as I could an' stayed there till dark. I'd like to meet that flyin' critter now that I've got some size to me. If I could get a good strike at him, he wouldn't be botherin' no little baby rattlers nor baby copperheads in mah part of the mountains.

COPPERHEAD: Fang and claw, talon and beak, from deep seas to lofty peaks, both hunters and prey survive on Nature's land, but the deadliest killer of all is Man.

COTTONMOUTH: Copperhead is right. Man is a deadly predator. Take young timber rattlesnakes, for example. Although, it is likely that the chief cause of their deaths is freezing weather, for many young snakes get caught out in the cold before they can reach the safety of their dens. However, death at human hands explains the alarming decline in the adult populations of timber rattlers in recent years. Many venomous snakes die on highways, but many more are blown apart by guns or other instruments of death. A venomous snake will retreat when it encounters humans. However, snake bites do occur when we are startled, stepped on, or given no chance to escape. Thanks to antivenin, a substance that counteracts the effects of venom, only ten to fifteen people die of the eight thousand persons bitten each year by venomous snakes in the United States.

CORAL: I must admit, I'm impressed, Cottonmouth, by you and the others. Copperhead's poetry isn't as bad as I thought at first. In fact, some of it is ... er ... uh ... rather good. And Timber is certainly a unique creature. I've never met anyone quite like him. But, Miss Winifred, isn't it my turn to speak? I feel I've been polite and patient for long enough. Now, I demand that I be allowed to speak. I have much information to share about the magnificent coral snake.

TIMBER: Let him speak, Oprie, 'fore he busts a gut. He shore is a little feller, ain't he? Why, I've seen baby rattlers near 'bout his size.

OPAL: Go ahead, Mister Coral Snake. You have our undivided attention.

CORAL: Finally! Thank you, Miss Winifred. Timber Rattlesnake seems to be concerned about our sizes. We coral snakes know that size isn't everything, but I'm willing to discuss this matter. Mister Copperhead represents the smallest of the pit vipers found in North Carolina. Average adult copperheads vary from twenty-four to thirty-six inches in length. Bites from the copperhead are painful, but they are not considered life-threatening or very dangerous to man. Fatalities are practically nonexistent.

The average adult cottonmouth ranges from thirty to forty-eight inches in length. The record length for a cottonmouth is seventy-four inches. The cottonmouth is considered a dangerous snake. Fatalities have occurred from their bites, and survivors sometimes have crippled fingers or toes.

The adult timber rattlesnake averages thirty-nine to fifty-four inches in length, and our friend Timber appears to equal the record length of seventy-four inches.

TIMBER: I try to eat right, git to the den early, and I don't have no bad habits to speak of. I used to lay on blacktop highways for warmth in the early spring, but one ev'nin', I lost three rattles to a little bitty sports car. I don't lay on any road no more! Too dang'rous!

CORAL: I'm sure everyone is fascinated by your adventures, Timber, but if I may continue? There have been fatalities from timber rattlesnake bites. The snake is considered extremely dangerous.

And now to my kind, the beautiful coral snake. I am an elapid snake, and included in my worldwide family are cobras, mambas, kraits, and sea snakes. My family is well-represented in Australia, Southeast Asia, Africa, and South America. Of course, I am the only elapid snake found in North Carolina. The average coral snake is between twenty to thirty inches in length. The record length for a coral snake is forty-seven and one half inches. Many herpetologists classify the coral snake as the most venomous snake in the United States.

TIMBER: Jest listen to ye brag. Ever'body knows that the eastern diamondback rattler is the most pizen snake in North Carolina. One of them big diamondbacks can pump out a powerful, big dose of venom.

CORAL: Drop for drop, my venom is more potent than the venom from any of the pit vipers. My venom is chiefly neurotoxic, which means it affects the functioning of the nervous system, primarily the respiratory center. I have short, fixed front fangs which do not fold back, as is the case with pit vipers. Because I have a small mouth, I cannot easily bite a human. However, fingers and toes are vulnerable. When I bite, I must hold on and chew to get my venom into the bloodstream of my prey. I feed primarily on small snakes, lizards, and amphibians. Occasionally, I will take a little rodent. I often enjoy—

OPAL: Excuse me, Mister Coral Snake, but that's all the time we have for today's show.

CORAL: What? Out of time? But I have more to say ... .

OPAL: Each of you has given my television audience a wealth of information about venomous snakes found in North Carolina. I wish all of you a safe journey back to your natural habitats.

CORAL: But, Miss Winifred, I have just scratched the surface concerning the beautiful coral snake. I can tell you about many of my adventures in the wild. I hatched one warm day in late August. My red, yellow, and black colors gleamed in the autumn sunlight, and—

OPAL: I'm sorry, Mister Coral Snake, but we really must say goodbye.

CORAL: Oh, very well, Miss Winifred. What a pity we are limited by time. However, in spite of my frustration, I bid you a fond farewell, dear lady.

COTTONMOUTH: Goodbye, Miss Winifred, and thanks for airing this program about North Carolina's venomous snakes. My hope is that we can live on, undisturbed by Man in our natural habitats.

COPPERHEAD: The Bard of Avon said "Parting is such sweet sorrow." Would that Man might learn, on some bright morrow, that our wilderness world is shrinking fast. Only Man's good judgment can make it last. Adieu, Miss Winifred.

TIMBER: Thank ye, Oprie, for lettin' me speak mah piece 'bout rattlers. Yore awful nice an' awful purty. Next time mah mate births a bunch of little rattlers, we'll name one of the little she-snakes "Oprie."

OPAL: Why thank you, Timber, and let me remind our viewing audience that on tomorrow's show, our guests will include four mammals that are on the endangered species list. We'll be telecasting from the UNCG Auditorium on the campus of the University of North Carolina at Greensboro. Be sure to tune in. This is Opal Winifred saying "goodbye" from the Schaefer Center for the Performing Arts on the campus of Appalachian State University in Boone, North Carolina.

INTRODUCTION

TO SIV LANG SOV'S AUTOBIOGRAPHY

Now and then, English teachers receive assignments from students that they wish to share with the public. I received such an assignment from Siv Lang Sov when I was an English teacher at Ashe Central High School. The school year was 1984–85.

I had asked the students in my Advanced English II class to write their autobiographies—not an original idea, I admit, but it's an assignment that often inspires interesting writing. Siv, who was a former Cambodian refugee and a sophomore at the time, produced a paper with many grammatical mistakes. However, it was written in a powerful, simple prose style that obviously came straight from her heart.

Her life story was one of horror, hunger, and death, but it was also a story of love, faith, and the ultimate strength of the human spirit.

Safe in America, young Siv still was frightened by any man in a uniform, thinking he might be a Red soldier.

Red soldiers had put many Cambodians to death. In nightmares, she relived the terrible things she had seen.

The *Winston-Salem Journal* published Siv's autobiography, and her story was picked up by a few North Carolina periodicals. I asked the *Winston-Salem Journal* to publish Siv's paper for two reasons. First, we American citizens—those of us who were born in this country and may have taken our free society, public schools, and high standard of living for granted—may learn something from this young student born on foreign soil. Second, as an educator myself, I wanted to recognize the three teachers (all now retired) who Siv Lang Sov said had helped her the most: Jefferson Elementary School teachers Laura McConnell and Mary Tugman, and Ashe Central High School teacher Linda Lindsey. With the help of these Ashe County teachers and others like them, Siv had made remarkable progress in just a little over five years of schooling in Ashe County.

Siv Lang Sov is "Siv Ashley" now—an American citizen who is married to Kenny Ashley. She and Kenny have two children, Ty and Tia. Serving on a mission team, Siv returned to Cambodia on October 16, 2012. Her visit to Cambodia is documented in her book, *A Teenager's Survival: The Siv Ashley Story*. While in Cambodia, she met a man who was a former Red soldier and was currently a minister. He asked Siv for her forgiveness, and she forgave him. Siv granted her permission for me to print her story here, and I am grateful.

In the pages that follow, you will read the brief autobiography she wrote during her sophomore year.

THE AUTOBIOGRAPHY OF SIV LANG SOV
BY: SIV LANG SOV WITH HAROLD (HP) PHIPPS

I was born September 8, 1965, in a land of beauty named Cambodia. I was raised in the country with my two brothers and two sisters. When I was small, life was very good. As I got older, it was hard because of the war, which was going badly. At the time, I was about five or six years old.

I didn't go to school because, in Cambodia, children didn't have to go until they were ten years old.

We had a large farm, and Papa worked every day. Mom stayed home, but, sometimes, she worked outside a little. When night came, Mom and Papa would tell old stories to us. They told us stories about Jesus and, of course, we believed in the Lord Jesus.

I woke up every morning to feed the chickens, pigs, ducks, and horses so I could run off and play with my friends. After I played, I helped around the house a little and ran off to the movie. Everything for us was good until the war started.

Suddenly, on October 3, 1975, the Red soldiers just came in and took our clothes and food away and told us to get out of the house. I saw the soldiers didn't care who you were—children, women, or men—they shot them all if you didn't do what the soldiers said. At the time, I was only nine or ten years old. We were sent off to the mountains and woods. The soldiers made us work and build our home in the forest. They also made us leave our parents. Children between seven to thirteen worked in one place. Children between the ages of fourteen and eighteen went far away to work in the rice fields and river digs.

We had ten people in our family—my grandmother, father, mother, two brothers, two sisters, my aunt and her daughter and me, of course. I was separated from my family to work in the fields with other children. Months went by, and people started dying because the soldiers didn't feed us right. They gave each person a cup of water and a cup of rice to eat, that was all. But they made us work day and night. We had only about five hours to sleep.

Finally, I got to come back to my family. When the time came to go back, my little sister had died. She starved to death. Everyone began slipping away, one by one, some from hunger, some from sickness. The next person to starve to death was my aunt's daughter and then my aunt. Then my grandmother, who was only fifty-seven years old, died. One of my other sisters and my youngest brother died because of sickness. My mother died without saying a word to me. She died suddenly and happy in my dad's arms. I can still see my dad crying and tears coming from his eyes.

My father didn't care much about anything after Mom's death. Then my father began to teach me about the things in America. He told me about the American people, and he said American people believe in Jesus Christ. He told me to pray and help other people in every way I could. He told me to believe in one God and I would go far.

My father told me, time after time, to find my other aunt and stay with her and go to America and get help for other people. My father did anything to get food for me and my brother to eat. He said to me, "You are young, and you can run fast." So, when the time came, he told me to take my brother and run.

But days went by. My father began to get sick. He was so ill, he couldn't walk. He lay in the grass bed where we built our home in the forest. I went off to find some food and medicine, but the soldiers caught me and asked me where I was going. I told them I was going to find my brother. I had to lie because if I didn't, they would kill me. I got back with some food, but I didn't find any medicine. My father told me not to go out anymore. He was afraid I might get killed, but I did it anyway to keep my father alive.

But, one day, a sadness came. It was a September morning with cool air. My dad woke me up and told me it was time for him to go. He told me that as soon as he was gone, I must take my brother and take the roadmap he had drawn for me. I was crying, and my dad told me not to. He said I must be strong. It was about 6:30 a.m. My father passed away. I saw tears from his eyes. I cried and cried and closed his eyes. I took my brother by the hand and told him our father was gone.

My brother and I buried our father. I didn't even have any tools to use to dig the ground with. I had to use my hands to dig. By the time we were finished, it was about nine or ten o'clock at night. My brother and I took off with some pictures of our family and some water and rice. We ran for miles and miles, and my brother got tired and rested a little. Then we met some other people who were running away too. So we followed them. It took days to walk across the mountains. We traveled by night so it would be cooler. But my brother got very sick. I waited in the forest until he got better. But he never did. We ran out of food. I had to climb trees to get food and kill frogs to eat.

My brother was dying. I tried everything to save him, but, every day, he slipped further away. He died, and now I was alone, scared, and hungry. But I kept hearing what my father said to me and what he taught me.

Time went by, and I was alone—no family—for two years. I helped a lot of people. Some were old, and some were only babies. I saw things I had never seen before. Things like people getting killed by having their heads chopped off and bones lying in big holes. A mother had to kill a newborn because she didn't have any milk and the baby would make noise. The Red soldiers would have found us.

One afternoon good news came, one of my father's friends found my other aunt for me, so, at that time, I stayed with her as my father had requested. We traveled together. We reached the far mountains and, finally, we got to Thailand. But the people in Thailand wouldn't let us in. Instead, they sent us back to Cambodia. But we decided not to go, so we stayed in the mountains about two months. Some people went back to Cambodia, some stayed.

About one thousand of us who stayed got to come to America. It was lucky for us. The American people flew planes, looking for us because they heard about us being sent back to Cambodia. American people sent foods and supplies for us. Then we came to America on a plane. Everybody was on the planes. By the time we got to Jefferson, North Carolina, I knew my father had been with me all the time.

Now, today, I am in the tenth grade and speaking English and learning French. I hope that, someday, when I graduate, I can become someone who helps people if I can, just the way my father wanted me to.

CALEB MONROE DINGLE TALKS TO GOD

During the late 1950s and early 1960s, many of the Baptist preachers in the Blue Ridge Mountain region considered themselves to have been "called" into the ministry. In other words, the voice of God had spoken to them and directed them to nearby Baptist churches, where they were to preach the gospel. As a youth, I always tried to believe what older people, especially preachers, said, but as I grew older, I had the uneasy feeling that, in some cases, the "calling" might've gone something like this:

***

"Caleb Monroe Dingle, this is God callin' on the telerpathic mind telephone. Yep, the mind phone inside yore head. I've been tryin' all mornin' to get through to you, but I kept gettin' a buzzin' sound like a busy signal from yore brain," said God, the All-Powerful. He sat down on a large golden throne and crossed His legs as

He modestly adjusted His glistening, snow-white robe. On either side of God's throne sat two large stone tablets upon which were written the Twelve Commandments. For reasons known only to God, Jesus, and the Holy Spirit, two had been crossed out, leaving only the remaining ten. Cherubs flew overhead, giggling as they chased after birds of many colors in the clear pink sky. Three bright suns, shining in the firmament, kept the temperature at a constant seventy-two degrees. As usual, the weather forecast called for a cloudless day.

Near God's throne, Jesus and the Holy Spirit rested on smaller platinum thrones. Actually, the Holy Spirit hovered around His throne like a glowing rainbow mist, a warm multicolored fog. An angel named Gabriel sat at Jesus's feet, tooting on an antique horn. Close by, an angel named Solomon, who had been a king back on Earth, sat under a golden tree with silver and bronze leaves. He was reading a physics book and humming to himself. Solomon leaned back, positioning his wings like large pillows against the tree of gold. A gilded walnut fell from the tree, joining several of its shiny fellows to rest on the newly mown bronze grass.

"Great gobs of goose grease! I just found another mistake in this here high school physics book," said Solomon to no deity in particular. He adjusted his halo, which had slipped down over his forehead. "Mankind ain't never gonna land on the moon unless they get a whole lot better at physics. I'm proposin' another commandment: 'Thou shalt take physics in high school.' And that means ever'body, girls and boys alike."

"Fellers, hush! Quieten down! I finally got through to Caleb Monroe Dingle on the mind phone. Y'all are goin' to have to be still so's I can hear him. That goes for you too, Gabriel. Put that dadgum horn down and quit messin' with it," said God as lightning flashed out of His left ear, showing He meant business. "Now, ever'body, be quiet!"

Jesus and Solomon bowed their heads, and the Holy Spirit's haze turned a soft shade of springtime green with thousands of tiny, floating red spots. Gabriel frowned but stuck his horn back inside his white robe and silently flapped his wings. Solomon ruffled his glossy feathers, opened his physics book, and continued his reading in silence. Jesus lifted His head and quietly sliced five large loaves of whole wheat bread and then began making tuna fish sandwiches for everyone—except the Holy Ghost, who preferred smoked turkey on rye.

"Caleb, are you still on the line? It's Me, yore Heavenly Father, wantin' to talk to you."

"Howdy, God," said Caleb Dingle, a lanky farmer whose family had lived for a number of generations in the North Carolina mountains. "I was just now thinkin' about You inside my noggin. No foolin', I surely was. Prob'ly the reason You got a busy signal earlier was that I've been out here hoein' corn all mornin' in the hot sun, sweatin' like a durn plow mule. My mind musta went on automatic pilot. You see, I've been workin' my goldang rear end off, pardon my French. I didn't mean to snap at You, God, but I've been milkin' cows, plowin' fields, pickin' beans, sloppin' hogs, and feedin' chickens, not to mention all my other chores. I'm plumb wore out,

God. Tomorrow, I got to get up when the rooster crows and start all over again. I'll be tuckered out again come sundown. To beat it all, I've done wore out two pairs of ole brogans this spring and here I am hoein' corn barefooted! It's a hell of a life I'm livin' on this rocky farm. The gravelly soil won't grow doodly squat. It's enough to make a'body cuss. There's gotta be a better way to make a livin'."

"That's the reason I'm callin' you, Caleb," God said. "I have done talked it over with My boy, Jesus, and the Holy Ghost. Of course, that horn-playin' smart aleck, Gabriel, had to put his two cents in, not to mention ole man Solomon. I got a truckload of Solomon's advice yesterdy. He couldn't wait his turn like any ordinary, God-fearin' angel because of him bein' a king once upon a time. He thinks he's so dang smart and wants to be consulted on ever' little decision that I make nowadays. Of course, him and Gabriel knows the final deciders is Me—Almighty God—My boy Jesus, and the good ole Holy Ghost."

Caleb wiped his brow, picked up his water jug, and took a swig. The water, having been warmed by the sun, was not refreshing. There was a static buzzing in his brain, but he could still hear God's voice.

"Therefore, verily I says unto you that just yesterdy, We—that is to say, the Big Three—all agreed yore the man for the new post, so I got a job offer for you," said God, the Omnipotent. "I figger yore a purty good feller, Caleb, not countin' that time you took yore cousin Peggy Sue out behind the barn, and you kids showed each other yore privates. Of course, I done forgived both of you for that little incident. 'Young people will be young people' is what I always says. They ain't much mamas, daddies, or Me can do about it. Just raise young'uns the best you can, I reckon. Even My boy Jesus was a handful durin' His teenage years 'fore He got aholt of Hisself and begun to straighten up and fly right. In the New Testament, Me and His disciples left out all the stories of His wild teenage days. You see, the boy developed a little drinkin' problem around eighteen years of age, and the young'un was forever turnin' water into wine. Like any daddy would do, I worried about Jesus and prayed for Him many a night. I reckon I musta answered My own prayers. By age twenty-one or thereabouts, Jesus righted Hisself, give up drinkin' and skirt-chasin', and begun doin' good deeds like raisin' the dead, feedin' the multitudes, and causin' the blind to see.

"Anyways, I'm right well pleased with the way Jesus turned out. He's a purty good ole boy. Ever'body says so. I can't find no fault in Him nowadays. But I ain't callin' to talk about Jesus. What I'm callin' about is yore new job."

"God, I'm so busy now with farm work," said Caleb, scratching his head. "I couldn't take on no more responsibilities. This here farm is takin' all my time. I got to get back to hoein' this corn field 'fore the weeds take over. I got to get busy right now if I want to get done 'fore dark. Call me again on Sundy. Call anytime. I'll be here at home all day—mornin' till night—just restin' up for the next work week. It's been nice talkin' to You, God. Amen, praise Jesus, hallelujahr, and goodbye."

"Now, dang it, Caleb, don't hang up till you've heard My offer. I ain't in the business of callin' just anybody, so listen up and listen good, or I'm liable to toss a few lightnin' bolts yore way," said God, all mightily.

Although the skies were clear, there was a rumble of thunder through the valleys of the Appalachian Mountains. Lightning streaked across the blue sky. Caleb shivered in the sweltering sun. "Okay, God, I'm listenin'. You got my attention, but if it's all right with You, I'm goin' to keep hoein' corn while I listen to You inside my head. The weeds in this cornfield is dang near knee high, but I reckon You knowed that."

"Yep, I knowed about them weeds since I know everthin'. But My mind gets all cluttered up sometimes. It's awful hard to know everthin', 'specially when everthin' keeps a-changin'. Sometimes I get the goldangdest headaches. Thank goodness I created aspirin, Goody's Powder, and Carter's Little Liver Pills, but I didn't call you inside yore head to talk about weeds, aspirin, or headaches! I'm callin' about a job, a good job; and Caleb, if you take this new job I'm offerin', you can forget about all this here back-breakin' farm work. I'm gonna reduce yore workload considerable."

"Tell me 'bout the job," said Caleb, wiping sweat from his brow.

"In yore new job, you will work mainly on Wednesdy nights and Sundys. You will have to visit sick people at home or in the hospital, and you will have to conduck funerals and say good things about the dead people, no matter how bad them folks was in life. Some of them dearly departed souls will be headin' straight for Hades in a hand basket, but you can't tell their grievin' families that. It wouldn't be the Christian thing to do."

"I don't hold with speakin' ill of the dead, anyways," said Caleb. From above and unseen, God smiled down on Caleb. A cooling wind bathed his face and birds chirped in a nearby cherry tree.

"Once in a while, Caleb, you might have to marry people. Some of 'em will stay married, and some of 'em won't. Nowadays, it's like flippin' a coin—heads they get a divorce or tails they don't—so don't worry yore head about it. Mainly, you will have to preach the gospel to yore congregation in a Baptist church ever' Sunday."

"Now, hold it right there, Lord. I'm deathly scared of gettin' up in front of people and makin' a talk," said Caleb. "I almost failed eighth grade because I wouldn't get up in front of the class and give a book report. Besides that, sick people ain't exackly my cup o' tea. Not wantin' to catch no diseases, I stay away from sick folks as much as I can, and dead people give me the heebie-jeebies. Lord, have mercy, and don't put me into no job where I have to deal with no sick folks nor no dead people!"

"Don't worry, Caleb. After yore baptized in the waters of the New River, I'll take away all yore fears. And when yore preachin', I'll tell you exackly what to say, just like I'm talkin' to you right now inside yore head. Besides, most of the congregation won't be listenin' to you, anyways. Them that ain't sleepin', they'll be thinkin' 'bout other things, like how dry the weather's been, how much it would cost to trade up for a newer car, or how that purty teenage girl that sings in the choir is fillin' out and lookin' more like a fine young woman with ever'

Sundy that passes." The floating mist that was the Holy Ghost flashed gold and green and emitted bursting blue bubbles that gave off the scent of lilacs. The activity indicated laughter on the part of the Holy Spirit. God smiled and winked at the hovering fog.

"So when I'm preachin', You'll be puttin' the words inside my head so's I don't have to think much?"

"That's right. You'll be movin' yore mouth, but I'll be doin' the talkin'. Now here's somethin' important! If you and Me was to get cut off in the middle of a sermon, just start jabberin' till I come back on the line. That sumbitch Satan sometimes cuts Glory Land's telephone lines, but don't you worry none, I can usually get things fixed in a minute or two. They don't call Me 'all-powerful' for nothin'. While I'm off the line, don't say nothin' that the congregation might understand, just babble, gabble, and blather, you know. Stomp around and pound yore fist on the pulpit a time or two. They'll think yore in the spirit and speakin' in tongues! Some church folks, bless their hearts, just love that kinda thing!"

"Lord, You say my work would be mostly on Wednesdy nights and Sundys?"

"Yep, most of it. Remember what I said about visitin' the sick, performin' weddin's, and preachin' funerals, and such. I might throw in a tent revival in the summertime, but most of yore work will be made up of preachin' on Sundys with a little dab of work on Wednesdy nights. Whoops, I almost forgot to tell you this: Be sure to have the choir and congregation sing a hymn or two before you pass around the collection plates. Singin' a good ole hymn loosens up ever'body's pocketbooks and billfolds.

Now, since I ain't got all day, let's get down to business. Will you take the job, Caleb?"

"Yes, I will. I surely will, and thank You for callin' me, Lord. I look forward to workin' for You," said the new preacher, Caleb Monroe Dingle. He was just about to hang up his mind phone when he heard the voice of God speak once more.

He also heard a horn tooting in the background.

"Hold on, Caleb. Don't hang up yet. What's that, Jesus? I didn't understand You, Son. Dang it, Gabriel, can't you quit practicin' on that infernal horn for just a little while? This here day-and-night horn blowin' is drivin' Me plumb crazy. I don't need no extry noise, Gabe. I got so many prayers, sermons, and voices spinnin' around inside My head, it's a wonder I can think at all. And My ears just ain't what they used to be a few centuries ago. What? Repeat that for Me, Jesus. Speak up, Young'un. Hmmm. Okay, okay, I'll tell Caleb," said God to His only begotten son.

"Does Jesus want to talk to me?" asked Caleb, flattered. "I've always wanted to have a little talk with Jesus, you know, kinda tell Him all about my troubles and see if He has any answers or ideas to help me out."

"Nope, Jesus just wanted Me to tell you not to do nothin' He wouldn't do!" laughed God, slapping His knee. "Haw! Haw! Sometimes that Son of Mine thinks He's a genuwine comedian. Jesus can be a real card. He gets His sense of humor from His momma's side of the fam'ly, I reckon. That young'un cracks Me up at least once a day. He thinks He's a reg'lar Bob Hope or Milton Berle. 'Don't do nothin' I wouldn't do!'" God threw His head back and giggled like a second-grader. "Hee! Hee! Hee! That kindly narrers the field of what a feller can do, don't it? But don't worry, Jesus is just jokin' with you, Caleb. He don't mean no harm by it."

"Oh," said Caleb softly. "I reckon He don't want to talk with me."

God knew the farmer's feelings had been hurt, so He tried to cheer him up. "When Jesus and ole John the Baptist get together and commence to tellin' stories, tales, and jokes about the good ole days, Me and the Holy Ghost get so tickled that tears come to Our eyes. Well, that ain't exackly right 'cause the Holy Ghost ain't got no eyeballs. He's a spirit, don'tcha know, but when He gets real tickled, He turns a bright shade of yeller and little purple bubbles start poppin' outta His foggy mist. When the bubbles bust, the air smells just like roses. HG likes a funny story or a joke better than any spirit I ever seen.

"If you get up here to Heaven, Caleb—and I reckon you will pass through the Pearly Gates—have Jesus or John the Baptist tell you that story of the night when ole Noah got staggerin' drunk, fell overboard off the ark, and come within a eyelash of bein' swallered by a whale. That tale is a real knee-slapper. Ole Gabriel dropped his horn and almost laughed his wings off when he heard about Noah's fall! It's a right funny story, but My personal fav'rite is the joke about the cross-eyed mule in the watermelon patch that John the Baptist tells. The first time I heard it, I laughed so hard, I caused a big earthquake down yonder in San Francisco. Couldn't help it! Get John the Baptist to tell you that mule joke when you get up here amongst the angels. My boy Jesus is a heck of a storyteller, and John the Baptist ain't no slouch hisself!"

"I'll do that, Lord, when I get to Glory," said Caleb. "I ain't heared a good joke down here in a month of Sundys. I was just wonderin' what a'body does to pass the time up yonder in Heaven. Do You and the angels mostly just float around, sing hymns, and heap praise on one another?"

"No, Heaven ain't like that at all. We have fun, loads of fun. Heaven ain't borin'. For example, Jesus, His eleven disciples, and a few other players have a big baseball game today," said God. "Our boys is playin' Satan's All-Stars, mostly made up of New York Yankees, over at the Purgatory Stadium. When them Yankees fellers was alive, they was called 'damn Yankees' for a dang good reason, don'tcha know. I reckon playin' in New York City brung out the sinnin' nature in them Yankee boys. Big cities is always full of nightclubs, beer joints, loose women, and gamblin'. Once them Yankees commenced sinnin' in the Big Apple, they found it awful hard to stop, I reckon."

"I'm a Brooklyn Dodger fan muhself," said Caleb. "Listen to their games over the radio. The Dodgers has got a fine pitcher by the name of Preacher Roe. He went twenty-two and three back in 1951. Have You got any good pitchers on Yore team?"

"Well, I reckon so. Jesus throwed a no-hitter the last time He pitched. Made His momma, Mary, and Me mighty proud. He struck out Ty Cobb four times! You ain't never heard cussin' till you've heard the Georgia

Peach cuss! The score was nothin' to nothin' through eight innin's, but Heaven's team won in the ninth when our first baseman, Lou Gehrig, hit a homer off of Ole Scratch hisself. Lou hit a line drive into the right-field seats, knockin' the halos off two angels and a cherub. The cherub caught and hung onto the baseball. Lou autographed the ball after the game was over. That little freckle-faced cherub—We call him Cupid—was tickled to death," said God, scratching at a tangle in His silver beard.

"Wow! Lou Gehrig homered just like he done at Yankee Stadium!" exclaimed Caleb.

"Yep, ole Lou walloped the dickens outta that ball. I like that Gehrig boy, even if he was a Yankee. The ole Iron Horse led a mighty fine life down yonder on Earth. Now he plays first base up here in Heaven. Someday I'll have me a strong outfield of Willie, Mickey, and the Duke, not to mention Roberto Clemente, Ted Williams, and Stan Musial. Jackie Robinson, Roy Campanella, and Yogi Berra will be on our team one of these days too, I'm sure. I can't hardly wait, but I reckon them baseball players can. They got long lives to live, most of 'em. I don't want to rush them boys up here to Heaven just for some ballgames."

Caleb rubbed his chin and wondered if he should try out for Heaven's baseball team when he got to Glory Land. He picked up a clod of dirt, went into a pitcher's windup, and fired it into a fence post more than thirty feet away. His throw was accurate. The post trembled and the clod of earth disintegrated, leaving dust in the air. *I got a purty good fastball,* he thought to himself. *I reckon it wouldn't hurt to try out for Heaven's team. I hope the Lord was watchin' that pitch.*

Then God's voice crowded out his thoughts. "In the next game, which takes place this comin' Sundy afternoon, Judas is pitchin' for Satan's All-Stars; and John the Baptist is pitchin' for us, the Glory Land Gladiators. It'll be a heck of a game, Caleb. Wish you could be here!"

"If it's all right with You, I reckon I'll pass on that, Lord!" said Caleb. Caleb's hands trembled, shaking his hoe. "I ain't ready to go to Heaven … not yet. I got some earthly things I want to get accomplished. Mainly, I want to have me a wife and sev'ral children and raise up a fam'ly. Nope, I ain't ready to go to my Heavenly home."

"Yep, I understand," said God. "I reckon it's true: ever'body wants to go to Heaven, but nobody wants to die. I don't take no offense to that way of thinkin'."

"What happens after baseball season is over up yonder in Heaven?" asked Caleb, kicking at a cantaloupe-sized clod of dirt.

"Why, football season, of course. You know, Caleb, I like baseball, but I'm plumb crazy 'bout football. I can't wait for the season to commence. In the first football game, we're set to play Lucifer's Lions. Our team, the Holy Rollin' Saints, is gonna be real good this year, and next year, with some new recruits, the team is gonna be even better. Of course, that dadgum rascal Satan will get some purty good recruits too. He always does.

"This year, Little David will be the Saints' quarterback and Goliath is the fullback. Yep, ole Goliath made it up here to Heaven. You see, back on Earth, Goliath was a good ole boy at heart. He just fell in with the wrong crowd of Phillerstines. On Heaven's football team, his long, strong legs make him hard to tackle. And Lordy, can he run—dodgin' from side to side, jumpin' over tacklers, and spinnin' into the end zone for a touchdown. Yep, as far as football goes, the Saints has got a right good ground game, and the passin' game is fair-to middlin'."

"Heaven is soundin' better to me all the time," said Caleb, who, like God, was also a football fan. Caleb and his mother, Gracie Elvira Dingle, seldom missed a local high school football game.

His mother, a hefty woman, had died of an apparent heart attack after a game in which her favorite team, the Blue Ridge High School Ravens, had lost by the score of twenty-one to twenty. At the end of the game, she dropped her foot-long hotdog and french fries, spilled her ice-cold Pepsi, grabbed her ample bosom, and pitched forward, rolling and bouncing out of the crowded, wooden stands. Picking up momentum and speed, she crashed downward into a group of cheerleaders, injuring a senior girl's left ankle; bounced over a long bench, scattering the home team; and knocked down a referee who was standing on the sidelines near the fifty-yard line. Mrs. Dingle came to rest under the scoreboard where she lay still. There was a doctor at the game, but he couldn't revive Caleb's stricken mother.

"God, is my mama up there with You in Heaven?"

"She sure is. She's waitin for you, Caleb. You'll see Gracie when yore time comes. Right now, she's over at the cement pond, pickin' flowers. She always puts a bunch of flower baskets out to decorate our big supper table. She sets a mighty purty table, bless her heart, and I ain't never tasted nothin' better than her homemade bananer puddin'."

"Did Aunt Lou make it through the Pearly Gates?"

"Nope. Not by a long shot!" said God with a hearty belly laugh. "Yore Aunt Lou could outsin Jezebel and Delilah put together. That woman had so many sins, I couldn't hardly keep track of 'em all. Soon as I'd forgive one wrongdoin', she'd commit two or three more sins ten times worse than the first. I got plumb wore out tryin' to forgive all her trespasses. Yore Aunt Lou ain't here in Glory Land. When you get here, you needn't look for her, Caleb. She didn't make the cut."

Caleb sighed and said, "I didn't figger she would make it to Heaven. But I sorta hoped she would."

The farmer was quiet for a long time, so God decided to broach another subject. "Caleb, do you like fried chicken?" asked God. "The Holy Ghost—some people call Him the 'Holy Spirit,' I call Him 'HG'—wanted Me to be sure and ask you about that."

"Ain't nothin' better on God's … uh … *Yore* green earth than a fried chicken breast served up with hot buttered biscuits, sliced garden maters, mashed up taters, green beans cooked with fatback, and don't forget the sweet tea to warsh the good food down with!" said Caleb, the brand-new preacher. He rubbed his skinny belly.

"That's what I wanted to hear, 'cause you'll be eatin' a mess of fried chicken for dinner after church services on Sundys. I told Jesus and HG that you was the man for the job. Now I'm plumb sure yore the right feller. Well, I gotta go, Caleb. I got a whole list of mind calls to make and a bunch of prayers to answer ... and some to leave unanswered. Now you go on back to yore cabin and start readin' up on the Bible. I'll be back in touch real soon."

"Wait, God, there's just one more thing 'fore I take this here preachin' job Yore offerin'. Could You send me down some kinda omen or sign? I need to know I'm talkin' to the real God and not somebody pretendin' to be God inside my head. You can't be too careful nowadays. I don't want to be made a fool of nor flimflammed. I ain't askin' for much of a sign—how 'bout changin' this here jug of spring water into wine?"

Suddenly, there was a clap of thunder and a flash of lightning, after which all of Caleb's fingers became long, writhing copperhead snakes, and his toes became snapping-turtle heads, varying in size but all sharing a foul temperament. The snakes hissed and struck at each other, and the turtle heads snapped and clicked their hard jaws. After a few seconds, Caleb's digits changed back to his normal fingers and toes. "All right! All right! I'm a believer! Ain't no doubt in my mind! Glory be to You! Hollered be Thy name! Thy will be done! Murry Christmas, Happy New Year, and hallelujahr! Thanks for the call, and call me anytime You get a hankerin', Lord. Amen and goodbye!" cried Caleb Dingle.

"Bye, Caleb. It's been My pleasure talkin' to you. This is God signin' off. Ten-four, good buddy. Over and out!"

Caleb hung up the telephone inside his cranium, stopped hoeing the corn, and headed back to his cabin. From a desk drawer inside the cabin's main room, he pulled out the dusty Dingle family Bible, sat down in a rocking chair, and began reading the Good Book. "Let's see. I'll commence with the first book of Moses, called 'Genersis.' Mama always said, 'Begin at the beginnin', Caleb.' Bless her heart, she was most always right. Uh, here's a word I ain't never heard tell of. I wonder what does 'firmament' mean? I'll find me a dictionary and look it up later. I'd best keep on readin'. Well now, on this page, God is makin' the sun, the moon, and the stars. I wonder how He done it?"

After ten minutes of reading, Caleb's chin fell to his chest, and he began to snore. He dreamt of steepled churches with choirs singing hymns, of collection plates stuffed with five- and ten-dollar bills, and of Sunday dinners with platters heaped with fried chicken. The Bible slipped from his fingers and fell to the floor. One of Caleb's old hound dogs, Buttermilk, thinking Caleb might've dropped some food, came over and sniffed the Bible. Deciding the book wasn't edible and of no use to her, the old dog returned to her usual place on the mat beside the fireplace. Soon, both Caleb and the hound were sawing logs.

MY FRIEND,
COUNTRY JONES
PART I

I pulled my tricolored 1956 Mercury Montclair into the Central Ashe High School parking lot and parked next to my classmate Pudge Hawkins's 1954 Ford Crestline. I was a senior—class of 1963—at Central Ashe High School in Jefferson, North Carolina. Not far away was a larger town called West Jefferson. The region had two prominent landmarks—one was a river and the other was a mountain. The New River rolled northward through the County of Ashe, and Mount Jefferson stood like a towering sentinel guarding the towns of Jefferson and West Jefferson.

My Mercury was tricolored because of an accident involving its right front fender. From an auto junkyard, the previous owner replaced the dented fender but didn't paint the newer, undamaged fender the proper matching color. I bought the Mercury for a bargain price, but so far I, like the former owner, hadn't had the cash to paint the fender. My car had a mint-green roof and a dark-green body except for the navy-blue right front fender.

I turned off the ignition, and the engine sputtered, hiccupped, and wheezed before shutting down. The car's frame vibrated during shutdown with the final mechanical death rattle coming from a rusted muffler. I looked around the half-filled lot. Fellow senior John Bowman's red 1963 Corvair—an early graduation present—was the only new car in the lot. Most of the cars were like mine. They needed paint jobs, bodywork, and complete engine overhauls. Scattered among the cars were a few pickup trucks, and they were generally in worse shape than the cars. Country Jones's pickup truck, held together by congealed rust and black duct tape, hunkered down next to John Bowman's brand-new '63 Corvair.

Country's pickup had a rusty trailer hitch under the tailgate and an oil spill forming on the ground under the six-cylinder engine. The left taillight hung six inches off the ground. It was secured by several wires and a yo-yo string with the green, translucent yo-yo dangling behind and slightly below the taillight. The yo-yo almost touched the ground near the treadless left rear tire. The truck's right taillight was fastened to the fender by two twisted coat hangers. Three of the truck's tires were badly worn, but the front tire on the passenger side was a brand-new snow tire with deep tread. The truck had been hand-painted several times, and its original color was anybody's guess. The current color was Army green. I think the pickup was a Dodge, but it may have been a Chevrolet. Country Jones, however, insisted that it was "mostly" a Ford. The bug-spattered grill was heavily taped, and the tape had been painted over. The windshield, though, was spotless and the side windows were wiped clean. There was a small round hole in the pickup's hood.

A homemade bumper sticker read: *I may be slow, but I'm ahead of you.*

***

Last year, when we were juniors, I'd ridden home from the high school with Country Jones in his truck because my Mercury wouldn't start. I guess he felt sorry for me when he saw me in the high school's parking lot, kicking the Mercury's front bumper. School had been dismissed at three o'clock, and the parking lot was empty except for Country, me, and our vehicles. The time was 3:20 p.m., and I was cursing my car and its creator—the Ford Motor Company. I had an important date coming up with my girlfriend Sophia Bishop, and now I had a dead car. How could I have ever trusted a car produced by the company that had given America that colossal failure, the Edsel? Circling the car, I kicked each of the Mercury's tires.

"Well, if it ain't Hal Grayson. Havin' trouble, Hal?" Country Jones had drawled, pulling up beside my Mercury. His truck idled noisily, releasing noxious fumes through a juddering tailpipe, but a light breeze carried the exhaust vapors away into the woodlands near the school. Country turned the truck's ignition off and exited his truck to stand beside me.

"My Mercury won't start, Country. I pumped three-dollars' worth of gas into her yesterday, so she's not out of fuel."

"I reckon not."

"I need to get this car running before tomorrow night. I've got a date with Sophia Bishop. Tomorrow's her birthday. I'm supposed to take her out for dinner at Greenfield Steak House. I've already made the reservations. What do you think, Country? Can you fix this car? I sure would be grateful."

Country smiled at me through constellations of freckles. He removed his worn Western-style straw hat and scratched his rusty, auburn head. A yellow jacket landed on his hat and began crawling around its brim. He flicked it off, and the insect buzzed away. Country Jones had the smell of dry hay and barn-cured tobacco about him. Although the weather was warm, he was dressed in a blue flannel shirt, bib overalls, and brogans. He gave a token look under the Mercury's hood and then lowered it until the hood crunched shut. "I can just 'bout guarantee that you can keep your date with Miss Sophie. You see, nine times outta ten, in a situation like this, it's just the bat'ry and nothin' serious. I ain't got no jumper cables, or we could fix you right up. If your Mercury was a straight shift, I could push you, and we could get your vehicle started. But it ain't a straight. It's one of them automatics."

"Dang it! I wish that you had your jumper cables, Country."

"Me too. The reason I ain't got no jumper cables is 'cause some good-for-nothin' sumbitch done stole 'em.

The thievin' varmint broke into the Jones fam'ly garage and got up in the bed of my pickup truck and found my big toolbox. It was mighty strange, though."

"Why?"

"The crook didn't take nothin' but the jumper cables, didn't take none of the tools, didn't take my set of chains for winter drivin', and didn't take the brand-new snow tar, which I'd laid in the bed of the truck. The feller musta needed them jumper cables real bad. Didn't take nothin' else. I don't never expect to see them jumper cables again. It bewilders me why he just run off with them and nothin' else. Durn thief'll prob'ly get away with it too. Law enforcement in this county is mighty slack. Dammit! God da ... Whoops. I'm so put out about them stole jumper cables that I almost took the Lord's name in vain. I got to watch that. Whew!"

"Maybe the thief saw a light come on in your house or stirred up one of your dogs. He just grabbed the closest thing and made a run for it."

"Prob'ly," said Country. "I'm still mad about it. I can't abide a thief. Can you, Hal?"

I started to tell Country that Grandpa Charlie Franklin—my grandpa on my mom's side—once told me any man would become a thief if he or his family got hungry enough. Instead, I smiled and said, "'Thou shalt not steal.'"

"Yep, that's the eighth Commandment, Hal. I learnt that in Sunday school. And I think it's one of the best Commandments that Noah brought down from the Mount of Olives."

"Huh?"

"Noah is my fav'rite Bible character, not countin' Jesus. Accordin' to what I've learnt in Sunday school, Noah is all over the Bible's pages, getting' swallered by a whale, helpin' the Christians tear down them Jericho walls, and leadin' the Philerstines out of the Promised Land. Not to mention turnin' Lot's mother-in-law into a salty pillar. But I reckon the big flood and his handlin' of it is what makes him my fav'rite Bible feller."

Country Jones swatted at another yellow jacket that kept buzzing around his head. The yellow jacket then began dive-bombing me. Two more yellow jackets arrived. Country and I spun around, waved our arms, and clapped our hands. Between the two of us, we managed to scare the wasps away.

Country turned back to me. "My mama and daddy thought about givin' me the name of Noah 'cause it was rainin' mighty hard the night I was birthed. Daddy said the creek beside our cabin jumped its banks and come splashin' up to our big log doorstep. The New River flooded its banks and warshed away the Worth family's outhouse, which was unoccupied at the time, thank goodness. The Worths is our closest neighbors, but our outhouse, praise the Lord, wasn't bothered none.

"I was birthed at home like all us Jones young'uns was 'cause Daddy don't believe in no kinda horspitals. Daddy Jones says horspitals is for rich folks that has insurance, jobs, TVs, and stuff like that. Ever'thin' all boils down to money accordin' to Daddy. You either got cash, or you ain't. We ain't got much money in the Jones fam'ly. Hal, did you ever wonder how Noah, livin' in them olden times, got the cash to build that big ark?

Did you ever wonder was Noah a rich man or did he borry the money to build that big ole boat? Did you ever wonder about that?"

"No," I said. The thought of Noah's financial assets had never crossed my mind.

"Me neither, never give it a second thought. But in thinkin' 'bout namin' me Noah 'cause of the flood on the night I was borned, Mama Jones said that nobody on her side of the fam'ly was named after Ole Testerment Bible people. Daddy Jones couldn't think of nobody on his side of the fam'ly named after Bible people neither, 'cept for Daddy's great-uncle, Solomon Jones, who turned out to be a fine moonshiner and a halfway decent horse thief."

"Moonshiner and horse thief?"

"Yep, Uncle Solomon Jones was a money-makin' moonshiner, and he was purty good at horse thievin' too. Mama said he was a big, stout feller, over six foot, five inches tall, redheaded like me and your pal, Pudge Hawkins, and awful big-boned. Uncle Solomon claimed to have stole over one hunderd horses durin' his twenty-five years in the horse-thievin' bizness. In his best year, he stole fifteen horses, two mules, and a pony. Uncle Solomon coulda stole more horses, but he considered horse-thievin' as his part-time job. He spent most of his time makin' white lightnin', like Shade Barlow does now. He had ort to have stuck with moonshinin' and left the horse-thievin' alone 'cause he got shot."

"Shot?"

"Yep, he was shot off a horse which he was stealin' at the time, and was bad wounded. The bullet went in his back betwixt his shoulder blades, tore through one of his lungs, clipped his gizzard, and come out his chest."

"His gizzard?"

"That's what my fam'ly was told by another horse thief, Uncle Solomon's partner, Grundy Blevins, who was there at the scene of the crime. But Grundy got away from the Greenbrier County deputy sheriff and his posse on a stole mule. Uncle Solomon lived just long enough to be hung from a tree up yonder in West-by-God-Virginia. They didn't have no trial. They lynched him on the spot."

"Lynched him?"

"Yep, Grundy Blevins said that a man from the deputy's posse throwed a rope over a thick tree branch, put Uncle Solomon up on the mare he had been tryin' to steal, put a noose 'round Uncle Solomon's neck, and slapped that horse on its ass, causin' it to run out from under Uncle Solomon. The fall snapped his neck, I reckon. At least he didn't suffer for a long spell like some folks does 'fore they die. He died quick. That hangin' happened a long time ago. We got a ole faded picture of Uncle Solomon settin' in the saddle of a big white horse, which he stole from a black man named Toby 'Horseshoe' Grimes. He shot Mister Grimes three times and kilt him down in Allegheny County. Daddy said back in Uncle Solomon's day, horse-thievin' was cornsidered a whole lot worse than shootin' a black man. Uncle Solomon turned out so bad that Mama and Daddy decided not to give me no name from the Ole Testerment. They figgered a Ole Testerment name might bring me bad luck and a early death, like it done poor ole Uncle Solomon Jones."

"Shot and hanged within minutes. That is bad luck."

"Real bad luck. Say, Hal, you ever heard tell of Goliath from the Bible?"

"Sure."

"I was borned a very big baby, and Daddy Jones thought 'bout namin' me 'Goliath,' but Mama Jones wouldn't hear of it. 'What kind of name is that to put on a child, Fonzie?' she asked Daddy. 'With a name like that, the other childern would laugh and make fun of him at school. Besides, the name Goliath comes straight out of the Ole Testerment. Mark my words, Fonzie, we ain't namin' this big baby Goliath.'

"I'm glad they didn't name me Goliath, but speakin' of big people, I had a uncle on Mama's side of the fam'ly, who growed to be over seven foot tall and weighed close to three hunderd pounds. He's dead now and buried in a special-made coffin."

"Seven feet tall? He was almost as tall as the basketball star Wilt 'The Stilt' Chamberlain."

"Yep, my uncle took the seat out of his pickup and put in a low bench just so's he could fit in the vehicle. The name 'Goliath' woulda fit Uncle Smith Pruitt, who was sometimes called 'Too Tall' Pruitt. He died young, only forty-two, in a sawmillin' accident. A tree he was cuttin' down fell on him and struck his head. He run away from the fallin' tree, but it done no good. If he had been a foot shorter, the tree limb that hit Uncle Too Tall Pruitt on the back of his head mighta missed him, or so the sawmill men said. I'm glad that Daddy and Mama didn't name me Goliath, nor Noah, but even Noah woulda been better than Goliath. Besides I ain't no giant. I ain't much bigger'n what you are, Hal."

I nodded and declared, "Wow! My relatives are boring on both sides of my family when compared to your uncle Solomon Jones and your uncle Too Tall Pruitt. You know what? I think I'll start calling you 'Noah' instead of 'Country.' I'll get my buddies, Tank Banner and Pudge Hawkins, to call you 'Noah' too."

"You better not, Hal!" laughed Country Jones, splitting a sea of freckles with his grin. "The name 'Country' suits me fine 'cause you ain't gonna meet many folks more *country* than what I am."

Country Jones was right. He would've fit in with TV's Clampett family, which included Cousin Jethro, Elly Mae, Uncle Jed, and Granny. The Clampett clan— poor country folks who had discovered oil on their land, making them rich—appeared weekly in the hit television show, *The Beverly Hillbillies*. After one episode, my grandfather, Morgan Grayson, wondered aloud if some mountain people might be offended by the show, which poked fun at hillbillies, mountaineers, and country folk.

After watching a few episodes, I had decided that mountain people didn't take offense because the show emphasized Jed Clampett's honesty, family loyalty, and common sense. One character on the show intrigued me more than the others: Elly Mae Clampett. Elly Mae, who could beat her big Cousin Jethro Bodine in a "rasslin'" match, was innocence in tight blue jeans. In one episode, the naïve Elly Mae thought a brassiere was a "double-barreled slingshot." My mind wandered with pictures of Elly Mae Clampett in her snug blue jeans flashing through my teenage brain.

My daydreams of Elly Mae continued until Country Jones's voice brought me back to reality. "Yessir, Noah is my fav'rite Bible character, 'cept for Jesus, and I'll tell you why. Hal, did you know that Noah saved the whole wide world? If it wasn't for Noah, no person nor animal would be livin' here on this earth right now. Ever'body's ansisters and ever'thin's ansisters woulda been drownded."

Country's words took me back in time. When I was six, I had a Bible coloring book. The book was a Christmas gift from Grandma Trula Grayson. One of the pages had a picture of the ark with the animal pairs on board. I liked the giraffe pair and Noah with his long hair and beard. With a green crayon, I colored Noah's hair and beard. Remember, I was just a kid. I then colored the two giraffes red.

"Tell me more about Noah," I said.

"When I was a little boy, my Sunday school teacher, Deacon Garland Kyle Ross, told us young'uns how Noah parted the Red Sea and helt back the water after it had rained for forty days and forty nights."

Grandpa Morgan Grayson and I knew Garland Ross. He worked as a mechanic at the Ford place. Grandpa said that Mister Ross, like many men his age, had dropped out of school to find work. Garland Ross was thirteen when he stopped going to school. He "found Jesus" in his late twenties and eventually became a Sunday school teacher at Bear Creek Baptist Church.

"Accordin' to Mister Ross, ole Noah split the Red Sea so a pair of ever' critter on the earth, one male and one female, could slip through and climb to the higher, dry land up yonder near the top of Mount Parnassus, also knowed as 'Flat Top Mountain.' Noah done that so that all the animals wouldn't be drownded in the cold waters of the Red Sea. But before he done that, Noah built hisself a ark, which is a great big boat, and put his wife, young'uns, and kinfolk on board. He put his dogs and cats on board too. I know I woulda done the same. Then he loaded up the ark with as many animals as he could, two by two, one male and one female till the ark was plumb full of ever' animal that swims, runs, crawls, or flies."

"The ark must've been huge."

"The ark was three-hunderd-cubes long and one-hunderd-cubes wide, so he had plenty of room for a bunch of animals, except maybe for the two elerphants and the two hippypotamuses, which mighta felt crowded from time to time."

"Cubes?"

"Yep, I figger one cube was as long as two football fields and ten times wider than the New River."

"That's gigantic, Country."

"Yep, it was a purty big boat, but it had to be to hold all them animals."

"But what about the parting of the Red Sea?"

"As soon as the rain commenced to fall—and it turned out to be a gully warsher—ole Noah, carryin' his umbreller, left the ark, waved goodbye to his wife and fam'ly, and run over to the Red Sea. He kneeled down and prayed to Jesus: 'Jesus, how 'bout helpin' me save a whole bunch of animals and a few good people?'

"And Jesus said, 'Don't mind if I do, Noah. You're a purty good feller, accordin' to Daddy, and I ain't busy right now. Listen close, and I'll tell you how you can save 'em.' Ole Noah listened to Jesus's directions. Then Noah got up and clapped his hands three times and snapped his fingers twice, like this. Then he grabbed up a blacksnake, which was crawlin' at his feet. The snake turned into a steel rod, which Noah helt out over the waters. He hollered four times, just as loud as he could, 'Praise the Lord, keep the commandments, and count your blessin's!' And lo and behold, the waters of the Red Sea parted, allowin' more animals—amongst the many critters was one pair of alleygators and a pair of rhinosyhosses—to cross over to the dry land on the flat mountain top. The critters was gettin' soaked from the rain, but they was safe, and so was them what was on the ark."

"You're saying that Noah had two ways of saving the animals? One was parting the Red Sea, and the other was building the ark. I'm not sure that I believe—"

"When the animals got to the other side of the divided Red Sea, they was free to run and jump around and play on the mountain. Noah seen that all them animals was out of harm's way, and he was thankful, but it was still rainin' mighty hard, so Noah kept holdin' back the Red Sea. Meanwhile, Noah's Ark was bobbin' up and down in the sea like a wine bottle cork throwed into the New River rapids. On the evenin' of the thirty-ninth day—or maybe it was the fortieth day—of the big flood, the rain had begun to slack off, and Noah seen a big rainbow shinin' in the sky. Then Noah let the waters of the Red Sea come back together with a big, outlandish splash. He throwed the steel rod to the ground since he didn't need it no more. The rod turned back into a blacksnake which hissed and struck at his feet a time or two before crawlin' off.

"The next mornin', the sun come out, and after sev'ral days, the sunshine dried up the flooded land. Ole Noah was plumb tuckered out, but he set out to find his ark. He found the big boat settin' on top of a mountain, and ever'body, includin' all the animals, was safe. Noah opened a door on the big boat and out rushed a pair of skunks, follered by a pair of bobcats, follered by a pair of buzzards, follered by a pair of porkypines, follered by a pair of platypussies. Then all them other critters—little and big—run, hopped, and crawled through that big boat's open door."

I knew Country Jones had Noah and Moses all mixed up, but I let it go. Still, I wondered how he'd gotten the two Bible stories so muddled.

"Yep, all the animals that Noah had saved was all now on dry land, and they begun to repopulate the earth with their kind. The critters did a good job of reproducin' theirselves 'cause, nowadays, animals is all over the place, 'specially in the woods 'round the Jones farm. Rabbits has done a awful good job of reproducin'. I might go rabbit-huntin' this evenin' if it don't rain. There's more rabbits and deers in the Jones woods than you could shake a stick at. Oh, Hal, I almost forgot to tell you. Drivin' to school this mornin', I like to have hit a deer. The critter run right out in front of me, and I jammed on the brakes and missed the deer by no more than a inch or two. I almost wrecked my truck. Slud my pickup halfway 'round and then backards again. Some of my tars is gettin' mighty slick."

I leaned back against the sunlit metallic warmth of my Mercury. Country propped himself against his rickety pickup truck. We relaxed, using the vehicles for support. "Not so fast, Country, what happened to the people and animals that didn't reach the ark or make it across the parted sea?" I asked, hoping to return Country Jones to his Noah narrative. He spoke in the Appalachian mountain dialect, and his baritone voice caused his words to flow as smoothly as creek water passing over submerged rocks.

"They all drownded, except for the fish, I reckon. The reason God sent the great flood was that mankind had turned into a bunch of triflin', no account white trash, and the other races of mankind was just as bad as the whites. Ever'body was playin' cards, goin' to beer joints, bettin' on horse races, dancin' the boogie-woogie, drinkin' moonshine whiskey, cussin' their neighbors, and smokin' cigarettes and big cigars. People had quit goin' to church and Sunday school. On Sundays, they just set on their front porch steps, thinkin' of new ways to get into devilment. I reckon the good Lord got tard of mankind's sin and that's why He made it rain for forty days and forty nights."

I wondered if all the whales, seals, and dolphins survived the great flood. I started to ask Country what he thought, but he was continuing his tale.

"As I done told you, if you was listenin' careful, on the evenin' of the fortieth night, or thereabouts, Noah was awful tard and wore out from holdin' all that Red Sea water back, so he dropped his steel rod, which—as I told you—turned right back into a blacksnake. Then Noah let the sea rush back together, drowndin' the animals and the people that didn't make it over to the dry land. It was only through the grace of God that Adam and Eve—naked as jaybirds—with Adam carryin' baby Cain and Eve totin' baby Abel, made their way through the parted sea. You and me wouldn't be here if Adam and Eve hadn't lived through the great flood. Think about it, Hal. Adam and Eve, the father and mother of all mankind, woulda drownded if it hadn't been for Noah. I don't think the Bible gives Noah the credit that he's due."

"I'm beginning to understand why Noah is your favorite Biblical character," I said, grinning. "By the way, what happened to the unicorns? I've heard that they were so silly—always frolicking around—that they just missed the boat. Or did Noah decide to leave them behind?"

"I don't take no stock in unicorns, and I reckon Noah didn't neither. Besides, who hankers for a cross betwixt a one-horned billy goat and a horse? Not me, nor none of my kin. The world is better off without them foolish unicorns. I can only fault Noah for one thing, Hal. Yessir, Noah made one bad mistake, and it don't involve no unicorns. I even mentioned Noah's slip-up to Deacon Garland Ross, when I was a little shaver. One Sunday, I talked to Mister Ross on the church's porch steps after church services was over. Mister Ross agreed with me. He sure did. My Sunday school teacher said, 'Nobody's perfect, son, not even Noah, I reckon.' Them's Deacon Garland Ross's exact words."

"So you and Mister Ross found fault with Noah for something?"

"Yep! Namely for savin' timber rattlesnakes." Country crossed his arms over his chest and shook his head. He closed his eyes and said, "Noah never shoulda let them dang critters through to dry land!"

Timber rattlesnakes were once abundant in the North Carolina mountains, but towns, highways, schools, and farms had pushed the venomous reptiles back into the more inaccessible mountain regions. I'd never seen a rattlesnake living in the wild, but when I was about six years old, I saw a dead timber rattler on the back of a man's pickup truck. I had to be lifted up to get a good look at the thick-bodied reptile. The snake measured almost six feet in length. I was amazed at how dark the lifeless rattler was, almost as dark as the slender blacksnakes, which were quite common in the high country. I had seen more than ten black snakes in the wild.

Blacksnakes were routinely road-killed in the summertime. The dark asphalt highways retained the sun's heat and provided warmth on cool summer days and nights for cold-blooded reptiles and amphibians. I had seen many squashed garter snakes, plenty of mashed toads, and two compressed copperheads, but I never saw a single timber rattlesnake flattened on the highway. However, Country Jones lived on a farm in one of the more remote areas of the county. I had no doubt he had encountered a few timber rattlesnakes in his young life.

In fact, the lofty mountain that rose up behind Country's house was called "Rattlesnake Mountain."

"Timber rattlers is about the orneriest critters I've ever run across in these mountains," said Country Jones. "Sometimes them snakes will strike at you without rattlin'. When they do rattle, the buzzin' sound is enough to send shivers up a growed man's spine. I never heard a soul say a good thing about a timber rattler. Noah shoulda knowed better than to let them poison reptiles through the floodwaters. When I get to Heaven, I'm gonna ask Noah about it."

"You're sure that you're going to Heaven, are you?"

"Yep, I ain't got no doubts about it 'cause I got the faith. How 'bout you, Hal Grayson? You got any doubts?"

"Plenty of doubts," I said. I didn't tell Country, but sometimes I doubted whether Heaven was a real place.

"Well, you ain't goin' to Heaven with all them misgivin's, but I can fix that."

"How?"

"I'll commence prayin' for you, so you can be up in Heaven with me."

"I wish you wouldn't, Country. There's no need—"

"Shucks, it ain't no trouble, Hal, and it might work. Besides, you ain't got nothin' to lose, and if my prayers work, you got a whole lot to gain."

I didn't argue with Country's reasoning.

* * *

Country Jones disliked rattlesnakes more than any other boy I had ever met. There had to be a reason. Country had never been bitten by a rattlesnake, but it turned out that one of his favorite uncles had been. "Years ago, Hal," he said, "a timber rattler bit my Uncle Poindexter Duncan Pearson on his right big toe. Uncle Poindexter, better knowed as 'Pine Pearson,' was barefooted at the time. Uncle Pine said the snakebite felt like two needles prickin' him on his big toe at the same time. He said he could feel it when the poison was squirted in just above his toenail. Then he looked down and seen the five-foot reptile. It was a good-sized timber rattlesnake, but the snake didn't even rattle to warn Uncle Pine."

"You're right. Sometimes rattlesnakes don't rattle," I said. "The snake probably thought your uncle's big toe was prey."

"Maybe so. Uncle Pine was hoein' corn with his wife, Aunt Ophelia, whose maiden name was 'Payne,' if I ain't mistaken. Along with 'em was their only child, Poindexter Duncan Pearson, Junior, better knowed as 'Little Pine.' Well, Uncle Pine kilt the offendin' snake with a hatchet that he was carryin' in one of the loops of his bib overalls. He flattened the varmint's head with the butt end of the hatchet and then whacked its head clean off. Well, Aunt Ophelia throwed Uncle Pine down on the ground and commenced suckin' the poison out of his big toe. She stopped suckin' on Uncle Pine's toe just long enough to catch her breath and to tell Little Pine to run to the house and get help. Then she started up again, suckin' on that snake-bit toe for all she was worth. She spit out the poison mixed with blood. The very next evenin', doctors at the Jefferson Hospital took off Uncle Pine's big toe with a scalpel knife. One doctor said that Aunt Ophelia's quick thinkin' and quick suckin' prob'ly saved Uncle Pine's life."

"Gosh! The toe may have been lost, but at least your Aunt Ophelia's quick thinking got some of the venom out of your Uncle Pine's toe," I said. "I'm surprised, though, that the doctors amputated your uncle's toe. Couldn't they save it? There must've been some concern about gangrene."

As I leaned back against the Mercury, I realized this was the longest conversation I'd ever had with Country Jones. I looked at my watch. The afternoon was slipping away, but I wanted to hear more about Pine Pearson and his snake-bitten toe.

"Uncle Pine's toe had swole up as big and red as a ripe tomater, and the doctors was afraid that the gangrene might set in any time. I seen his toe before they whacked it off. The skin on the tip of his toe was already dead with the flesh there turnin' as black as midnight in a coal mine. 'Better to lose one toe than the whole foot,' said a serious-minded but awful young doctor to Aunt Ophelia. I reckon Uncle Pine was lucky to live through that timber rattlesnake bite and lose only his big toe. Aunt Ophelia never let Uncle Pine hoe corn barefooted again whilst they was still married, I can tell you that. Hal, I'd ruther be bit by a dozen copperheads, all at the same time, than be bit by a single timber rattler."

"Twelve copperhead bites all at once might be deadly, Country."

Country Jones ignored my remark and continued the tale of his uncle's toe. "Uncle Pine kept his big toe preserved in a quart jar of pickle juice, under his bed, hopin' that someday modern medical science could figger out a way to reattach that toe to his foot. He showed his toe to me one time. It was monstrous big and purple, just floatin' around that pickle brine like a bloated catfish. The toenail was pitch black. But the pickle juice didn't do no good in the long run 'cause, fin'ly, Uncle Pine's toe flesh just melted in the pickle brine, leavin' only the toe bone and the black toenail.

"Uncle Pine poured the contents of the jar—toenail, bone, and all—into Horse Creek one Sunday afternoon. Aunt Ophelia, who was Uncle Pine's third wife, stood on the Horse Creek low-water bridge and said a prayer over that empty pickle jar, prayin' that Uncle Pine's toe would be waitin' for him up in Heaven. She prayed that Uncle Poindexter Duncan Pearson, knowed by most people as 'Pine Pearson' as I said before, would be made whole in body and mind once again. She prayed that he would be reunited with his big toe in Glory Land. That woman was awful religious, and Aunt Ophelia truly believed that Uncle Pine someday would be healed up yonder in Heaven. That's why my uncle walks with a limp, Hal. He ain't got no big toe on his right foot. Thank God Uncle Pine's alive and can do 'most anything he wants to. At least that snakebite didn't kill him. What did just 'bout kill Uncle Pine was when Aunt Ophelia run off and took Little Pine with her."

"Your aunt left your uncle? What happened?"

"Uncle Pine got plumb mean after he lost his toe. Started drinkin' purty heavy. Any man would, I reckon. Aunt Ophelia couldn't stand livin' with him and his temper and his drinkin'. Hopin' it would do him some good and maybe get him to quit drinkin', she tried to get him to go to a Alkyholics Unanimous meetin', but Uncle Pine wouldn't hear of it. He said, 'That organization is for fellers who wants to quit drinkin'. I don't.'

"His temper kept gettin' worse. He'd fly off the handle at the drop of a hat. Threatened to kill Aunt Ophelia and Little Pine sev'ral times. Pulled a knife on 'em. When she couldn't take it no more, she left him. She took Little Pine with her. Some says Aunt Ophelia run off with a travelin' carnival man who was nicknamed 'Snake,' of all things. That's what folks says. I wouldn't know nothin' 'bout that, but I do know that she's still gone and has been gone for some time now. Uncle Pine lost this toe, his wife, and his son in a two-year period of time. That's what drove him to commence drinkin' almost ever' day, I reckon. Some folks says he's a good-for-nothin', hard-drinkin' alkyholic, and I reckon he is one. He don't drink much moonshine no more. He likes fancy whiskey now, like Ole Grand-Dad, Jack Daniels, and Jim Beam. His fav'rite whiskey is the George Dickel brand. I ain't seen him lately when he ain't been 'bout half drunk."

"I have a few alcoholics in my family too," I said. "I think every family does."

"Well, as I said before, it's a wonder Uncle Pine can still do 'bout anythin' he wants to do on the farm, if he ain't too drunk, and it's also a miracle that he ain't dead from rattlesnake poison. Folks says ever dark cloud has a golden linin'. I reckon that's true in Uncle Pine's case. I'm sure glad he ain't dead. I pray for Uncle Pine ever' night, right after I pray for Mama and Daddy and my sisters. I prayed for Uncle Pine for over thirty minutes after I heard he got snake bit. The Lord answered my prayers and let Uncle Pine live. I heard tell of a Boone man over in Watauga County who got bit by a timber rattler and died the next day."

I knew that deaths from timber rattlesnake bites were extremely rare. Nonetheless, permanent damage to the tissues around the bite was common. I remembered learning in my high school biology class that timber rattlesnakes were dangerous pit vipers. On the other hand, copperheads, also pit vipers, were much less dangerous. Generally, copperheads were smaller and injected less venom. As a seventh-grader at Healing Waters Elementary School, I had enjoyed reading about venomous snakes, and through my reading, I discovered that the state of North Carolina had four venomous types of serpents: rattlesnakes—several kinds—copperheads, water moccasins, and coral snakes. In the mountains of North Carolina, there were only two dangerous snakes: copperheads and rattlesnakes. The cold mountain climate kept water moccasins and coral snakes away from Ashe County and neighboring mountain counties. Loggers, cutting down trees to take to the various sawmills in the county, often encountered timber rattlesnakes when they worked in remote regions. The timber from Rattlesnake Mountain remained uncut. Loggers simply wouldn't go into that region for fear of encountering rattlers.

"You're right, Country, timber rattlesnakes can be dangerous, sometimes deadly."

"So why in tarnation would Noah, a fine Christian man and a good fam'ly man, accordin' to my Sunday school teacher, let a pair of timber rattlesnakes pass through onto the dry land, whilst he helt back the waters of the Red Sea durin' the big flood? Don't you reckon any man that could hold back the Red Sea waters coulda stomped the life out of two timber rattlers?"

I remained quiet as Country Jones scratched his chin and pondered his timber rattlesnake question silently for a full minute. Finally, he shrugged his shoulders in frustration. Then he said, "Why Noah allowed them rattlesnakes to live and multiply beats the tar out of me, but as Mister Ross used to say, 'The Great Speckled Bird works in curious ways her miracles to perform.' The Great Speckled Bird stands for the church, Hal, and not just any church. The Great Speckled Bird stands for the Baptist Church and not any of them other crazy churches like them Methodists and them Presbyterians. Them Lutherans is also a wild bunch, just like them Catherlics, I'm told. And don't get me started about them Normans who live way out yonder in Utah!"

"Normans? I think you mean Mor—" I said, trying to correct Country, but he continued.

"Mister Ross said that a man of the Norman Church can marry two or three wives at the same time. If he gets tired of 'em, a Norman man can just run them wives off and marry two or three or even four more. When Daddy Jones is pickin' at Mama Jones, he'll tell her that someday he's gonna hightail it for Utah and join the Norman Church and then marry three or four young, good-lookin' women. Daddy said he would start a new fam'ly way out West. He don't mean what he said, though. Daddy Jones don't like to travel much. He's happy right here in these here mountains.

"My Sunday school teacher, Mister Garland Ross, said the only good thing about the Norman Church is that they have a good choir and sing a bunch of Christmas songs. I listened to some of that choir's music over the radio last Christmas. They sing real good. It's kinda like hearin' angels singin'. I think that choir goes by the name of the 'Norman Tally Wacker Choir.'"

"I think you mean the 'Mormon Tabernacle Choir,'" I said.

"I believe you're right, Hal. The name of them singers is the 'Norman Table Whacker Choir,' come to think 'bout it," said Country Jones.

"I read that the Mormon Church has the official name of the 'Church of Jesus Christ of Latter-day Saints.' A man with the simple name of Joseph Smith founded the church a long time ago."

"It ain't no use talkin' about different churches, Hal. Don't be wastin' my time or your breath. Mister Ross says that the Baptist Church is the one true church. He says ever' other church should be called 'The Hell in a Handbasket Church.' I reckon he's right 'cause, in my church, what we teach—above all else—is that you gotta have faith, and I mean everlastin' and unquestionin' faith in Jesus, His Daddy who is God, and the Holy Ghost. Jesus and his crowd, you know, them twelve disciples— 'cept for Judas—knows what is best for us Christians in our earthly lives. For example, Jesus said that us Christians ort not never be guilty of castin' the first stone at people who live in glass houses. That's a rule I live by. Fact is, I very seldom throw rocks at anybody's house, glass or otherwise. I used to, but I broke myself of the habit of bustin' out winders in ole, abandoned, run-down buildin's."

Country Jones bent down and picked up a penny that was resting beside the back tire of my Mercury. He stood up and looked for the date on the penny. He wiped some dirt off the coin.

"Nineteen hunderd and twelve. Dang, that's a ole penny," he said, then put the coin in his pocket. He beamed at me. "I bet Jesus and His disciples had a lot of fun hangin' 'round together, makin' up them parables to teach people lessons. I wish I coulda lived in them ole Bible times. Jesus mighta picked me to be one of His disciples. The twelve disciples that He did pick was mostly good ole boys, like you and me, 'cept for that lowdown rascal, Judas. I would subtract that sumbitch Judas from the twelve for understandable reasons. Yep, I would take away that Judas feller. Jesus woulda been a whole lot better off with just eleven disciples, not twelve, unless number twelve was a feller like me."

"Country, I'd be interested to hear all your reasons for subtracting Judas," I said, hoping to learn more about Country's theology.

Country Jones wrinkled his brow, and for a split second, I thought there was going to be a freckle avalanche across his face. Country's voice took on a serious tone. "First of all, Hal, you ort to know that the number twelve has been rollin' 'round inside my noggin all day. It started this mornin' when I first woke up. Whilst I was gettin' ready for school, puttin' my pants on, I dropped a penny and it rolled under my bed. I got down on my hands and knees and looked under the bed, and lo and behold, I seen ten more pennies that I had hid under the bed for safekeepin'. I had forgot about them ten extry pennies. I grabbed up all them eleven pennies and put 'em in my pocket. I said to myself, 'I wish I had one more penny 'cause it costs twelve cents for a pack of licorice candy.' With the penny I found layin' on the ground just now, I have twelve pennies, enough to buy some licorice candy at Goodman's Store this evenin'. I'm keepin' them twelve pennies in my left pocket. My right pocket has got a hole in it. 'Fore I left for school, Mama Jones sent me to the henhouse to gather eggs. I come back with twelve eggs in my basket. When I come back in the house and put the eggs on the kitchen table, I noticed that our ole grandfather clock had stopped tickin' at midnight last night. Both of the clock's hands was pointin' up at the number twelve. And you just seen me pick up a penny that was dated nineteen hunderd and twelve. Now, I ain't superstitious nor nothin', but signs is signs, and you can't just ignore 'em like the signs ain't there."

"I'll admit, you've had a strange morning," I said, "but I'm not ready to call Rod Serling of *The Twilight Zone* yet. Now remember, Country, I asked you about Judas, not the number twelve."

"Well, Hal, you know 'bout how that tattletale Judas told on Jesus to the Romanians, and then he took the thirty-dollars'-worth of silver, and all that other rigmarole and hassle caused by Judas—'bout some Romanian soldier gettin' his ear cut off with a sword when the soldiers tried to arrest Jesus for trespassin' in the Garden of Gethsemane. And quicker than a wink, usin' silver threads and golden needles, Jesus sewed that ole soldier boy's ear right back on his head, good as new, maybe better. The Romanian soldiers didn't show no gratitude to Jesus, though. They just grabbed Him up and took Him over to the mayor, Pontiac Pilot, who crucified Him on Good Friday. It was all that sumbitch Judas's fault, plain and simple."

"Are you saying that Judas alone was responsible for—"

"Don't bother me with no trivials, Hal," said Country with his eyes tightly closed. "For I'm thinkin' again 'bout the number twelve, which has been rattlin' around inside my mind all mornin'. Now, 'cause I took that lowlife troublemaker Judas out of the twelve disciples, which brings us down to Jesus and the eleven disciples, which adds up to twelve people, one of which was the Son of God. If you add in the Father, the Son, and the Holy Ghost, as any Christian feller would, the number pops up to fifteen. But wait a minute, let's get this right. Jesus and the Son is the same feller, ain't that right?"

"You're right, Country. My Sunday school Bible teachings agree with you. Jesus is the Son of God."

"The Son and Jesus is one in the same. Ain't no doubt about it. So that brings the number down to fourteen people. Yep, that's right, fourteen people. The number fourteen is rollin' around inside my head right now, but the number twelve is still there too, stronger than ever. Whew! I'm fixin' to get a headache. Wait a minute, God and the Holy Ghost ain't people to my way of thinkin', so take away God and the Holy Ghost."

"Wait. Tell me again why you're taking away God and the Holy Ghost?"

"Because them two, the Holy Ghost and God, ain't flesh nor blood. God and the Holy Ghost ain't human beans. They didn't come from Adam and Eve, so the number comes down to twelve people. Now, don't try to confuse me, Hal, 'cause I got lots of numbers flyin' around in my skull at the present time," said Country Jones. "I'm trying to make some sense out all these numbers bouncin' around in my brain 'fore I get a headache!"

"I'm just trying to follow your train of thought, Country, not confuse you," I said. "I got derailed a while back with your numbers. I'm back on the right track now, just a little slow. My thinking is slower than the old Virginia Creeper train hauling freight up through the mountains to the West Jefferson Depot."

"Okay, Hal, remember I'm countin' Jesus in with the people 'cause His mama, if I ain't mistaken, was Mary Magdalene, a woman of flesh and blood. And I throwed His Daddy and the Holy Ghost out, remember? That leaves me with twelve people—Jesus and his eleven disciples. Yes. All righty, now my head is all cleared up. The number twelve is the only number stuck in my noggin. The number twelve ain't botherin' me no more, thank goodness, but it must mean somethin'. I just ain't figgered out what yet."

"Country, couldn't all of these examples involving the number twelve—the eggs, the pennies, the disciples, and even the grandfather clock—be mere coincidences?"

"It ain't no coincidence that twelve is the exact same number of disciples that Jesus had when He was walkin' on water down yonder in the little town of Bethlehem, swaddlin' Hisself in them clothes He found in the manger, and castin' out demons over yonder in the Garden of Gethsemane."

"Demons? Are you talking about demonic possession?" I said, startled. I didn't believe in demonic possession or any of the fiends from down below, but I didn't want to get in an argument with Country Jones about the mythical creatures from Hades.

"Yep, in them olden days, demons could jump right down somebody's throat and take control over their whole bodies—brain, heart, liver, and gizzard, everthin'. People who had demons inside of 'em was called 'repossessed.' Repossessed people always acted kindly funny. Jesus and some other preachers, like the Pope and maybe Billy Graham, had the power to jerk a demon out of a person. Of course, Jesus was the best at the castin' out of demons. Mister Ross said that Jesus had just as soon cast out a demon as to look at one."

"I read somewhere that the casting out of an unclean spirit is called an 'exorcism,'" I said. "I think Catholic priests today can exorcise demons, if you believe in that sort of thing. Personally, I—"

"Yep, Mister Ross said that after Jesus exercised them demons out of demon-repossessed people, He flung them wicked, filthy spirits clear acrost acres and acres of desert land and over a bunch of high mountains till those devils landed right smack in the middle of the Sea of Galilee. Well, ever'body knows that demons and devils, like witches and warlocks, can't swim a lick, so Jesus drownded a bunch of them suckers. And since Jesus flung so many demons—which we all know come straight from the fires of Hades—into the Sea of Galilee, the seawater itself took on a strange color and started steamin' and boilin' and bubblin' like when your mama boils corn on the cob or taters on the wood stove.

"The scorchin' and sizzlin' seawater kilt everthin' for miles and miles around. It wasn't only the demons what got kilt. The scaldin', churnin' water's heat kilt all the catfish, crawdads, bullfrogs, and most of the rainbow trout. I take that back, for I remember now that Mister Ross said the hot water killed all the rainbow trout, ever' dang one of 'em."

"Now, wait a minute, Country. I believe you have—"

"That's why people give a brand-new name to what was wunst named the Sea of Galilee. Folks calls that body of water the 'Dead Sea' nowadays 'cause nothin' can't live in the awful salty water. The only livin' things you could find around that body of blisterin' hot water at that time was the Dead Sea trolls, which lived way back in the caves thereabouts. Them trolls—ugly little sumbitches they was—lived so far back in the caves that I calculate that the burnin' salty water didn't touch 'em. The Dead Sea trolls must've had some freshwater springs way back in their caves 'cause no livin' critter can survive by drinkin' water from a salty sea. Mister Ross said the

Dead Sea is almost pure salt like that lake out there in Utah where the Normans live."

"Mormons, Country, Mormons, and I think you mean the Dead Sea Scrolls, not the Dead Sea trolls."

Country ignored me and continued. "I reckon all that extry saltwater come from the dissolvin' bones of them thick-skinned devils and scaly demons and maybe a few witches and warlocks throwed in for good measure. Them evil critters was dead and gone, thanks to Jesus, but it ruint the water thereabouts. Mister Ross told us kids in Sunday school class that the only good trout fishin' over yonder in the Holy Land is in the River Jordan. But I'm gettin' off my subject, which was numbers in the Bible. I reckon I'll have to start all over again so you can understand it, Hal. You see, they was twelve disciples—"

"No! No, no, you don't have to start again, Country. Please don't. I think I understand," I said, hiding a note of desperation in my voice. I was beginning to hope that Country's theological lesson would soon be over.

"Okay, Hal, do you see how I started out with the number twelve and after doing all that addin' and subtractin', which I done all in my head, I ended up with the number twelve? The same number as the months in a year, the same number that makes up a dozen eggs, and the same number as the inches on a ruler. It's kindly amazin' 'cause I didn't have no idea where I'd end up when I started workin' with them numbers."

"It's amazing, all right."

"It's the same in math class. Mister Kean, the 'rithmetic teacher at Central Ashe, says he can give me a problem with numbers in it, and they ain't no tellin' what numbers I might come up with. Wunst, I come up with the number one hunderd and two thousand dollars and ninety-eight cents in Mister Kean's consumer math class."

"One hundred and two thousand dollars and ninety-eight cents?"

"That happened when us students was trying to figger out how much a'body would spend on gas, fillin' up in Boone, North Carolina, and drivin' down to Miami Beach, Floridy. Mister Kean put a bunch of numbers up on the blackboard to help us figger the problem out, like gas prices, miles per gallon, and mileage and such. They was a lot of dividin' and multiplyin' and subtractin' goin' on in that there problem. I did some of the figgerin' in my head and some on paper. Mister Kean said my number, one hunderd and two thousand dollars and ninety-eight cents for gas money, was the biggest number anybody had ever come up with while workin' on that partic'lar problem. I was right proud of myself and told him so after class. Mister Kean just smiled at me, patted me on the shoulder, and told me to get on to the next class. Mister Kean goes to my church and teaches a Bible study class for adults and ole people. Mister Kean is a purty good Sunday school teacher, but he ain't near as good as Mister Ross."

A robin landed on my Mercury's roof, and I shooed the orange-breasted bird away, but not before the harbinger of spring pooped on the center of my car's roof. Overnight rain, heavy at times, was in the weather forecast, so at least the robin's deposit would be gone by morning.

"Hal, I'm better with Bible numbers than I am with reg'lar numbers in the classroom. Granny Josephine Jones says I got a gift for workin' with Bible numbers 'cause I was born backards. That is to say, my head didn't come out of Mama Jones first. My ass did. When my head finally did pop out, my noggin had a birth caul over it. Granny Jones says that a baby born with a birth caul has a gift for music or numbers, sometimes both. Granny Jones says there's a book in the Bible called the 'Book of Numbers.' I ain't had the time to check out that book to be sure, but if they is a book about numbers in the Bible, it would just make my faith in my Baptist church stronger. Anyways, today, I'm stuck on the number twelve. I don't know why."

"Yes, you started with the number twelve, Country, and you ended with the number twelve. I feel I've witnessed a small miracle right here in the Central Ashe parking lot," I said, smiling. "Hallelujah! Rejoice, Dear Hearts! Praise the Lord and pass the ammunition! I'm a born-again numerologist!"

Country Jones grinned like a freckle-faced possum. My comment tickled him. He put his hand over his mouth to hold back a laugh. "Aw, you're just funnin' with me, Hal Grayson," he said. "I don't blame you. I'm just a ole country boy. I don't know much about nothin'. By the way, Hal, what's today's date?"

"The twelfth," I said. I wasn't sure at first, but when I thought about it, I realized yesterday was the eleventh because we had a trigonometry test. I had to admit, there were a lot of twelves floating around.

"Ain't that a coincidence," said Country Jones.

Did I hear sarcasm in Country's voice? I wondered.

"And how many days of Christmas is there in that Christmas song 'bout that pear tree and them maids a-milkin'?"

"Twelve," I said.

"And how many knights set around ole King Arthur's round table?"

"Twelve," I said, scratching my head.

"And how many pairs of ribs does a normal human bean have? You ort to recollect that from today's biology class."

"Twelve pairs of ribs. You're right. In today's biology class, we learned about the rib cage and the organs it protects."

"How many folks sets on a jury over at the Jefferson courthouse?"

"Twelve."

"Ain't that a coincidence too? What I'm attemptin' to explain to you is that we ort not never to question the Bible nor the signs that come down from up above. Not now, not never! I know that the Lord or Jesus is tryin' to send me a sign usin' the number twelve. What do you think, Hal?"

"I don't know. Maybe."

"Hold on! Hold on! Wait a minute! Now I remember. My girlfriend Maude's little brother, Durwood, turned twelve today. That little bread snapper is growin' up fast. The whole Pugh family will be celebratin' tonight. I was invited to the birthday party, but I slick forgot 'bout it till now. Maude ain't been to school all this week. Her Aunt Nellie Neaves is 'bout to birth a baby, and Maude has been lookin' after her for sev'ral days. But Maude will be at tonight's birthday party all right. Dang, I almost missed it, but now I won't."

Country Jones bowed his head, closed his eyes and whispered, "Thank you, Lord, for usin' the number twelve to remind me of Durwood's birthday party. Forgive me for takin' so long to figger it out. Daddy always says I musta been at the back of the line when brains was handed out. For a present, I'm gonna get little Durwood a Superman comic book and some licorice candy, but I reckon You already knowed that, Lord. Bless Maude, Durwood, and all the Pughs. Oh, and bless Hal Grayson and his Mercury automobile and his sweetheart, Miss Sophie Bishop too. In Jesus's name, I pray. Amen."

Country Jones raised his head and grinned at me. "I been talkin' to the Lord."

"I know," I said. I glanced around the school parking lot and noticed it was empty except for the three of us— me, Country Jones, and the Lord. However, more than likely, there were just the two of us in the parking lot— one guy leaning against a tricolored 1956 Mercury and one guy leaning against a rusty pickup truck.

**

To some extent, I envied Country Jones' simple but deep faith, and I enjoyed hearing him speak. He had a silky-smooth, easy-going voice; and, once, my girlfriend

Sophia Bishop had said, "I could just listen to Country Jones talk and sing all day." I had felt a surge of jealousy when she said that, but I put the hot feeling aside. She was right about Country's voice, so I didn't mind when he began speaking again about his faith, which had sprouted under the guidance of Mister Ross, his Sunday school teacher.

"One Sunday, Mister Ross told our Sunday school class 'bout a Bible secret that most growed-up Christians don't know. Now listen to what I'm about to say 'cause it's important, Hal. Did you know that Jesus Hisself, with some help from John the Baptist, wrote the Bible, both the Old Testerment and the New Testerment? When He wasn't out climbin' up mountains, givin' sermons, and feedin' the multitudes on two catfish and five stale biscuits, He was writin' in the Bible, mostly at night, I reckon. And when He run out of black ink, what do you think Jesus done?"

"I don't know. I don't even have a guess," I said truthfully.

"My Sunday school teacher, Mister Ross, said that Jesus just pricked His finger with a thorn and spilled out some of His blood and went on writin' as hard as He could, usin' His own red blood for ink and a turkey quill for a pen. To this day, you can find Bibles where the words of Jesus is writ in red. We got a Bible at home like that," said Country. His chest puffed up a bit.

"Yes, I've seen Bibles with the words of Jesus written in red," I said. Country Jones nodded several times in succession, as if I had, by my words, fully endorsed his and Mister Ross's theology.

Country Jones continued, "My Sunday school teacher said that Jesus kept writin' right up to the time when they kilt Him usin' them cross ties and a bunch of tenpenny nails in His hands and feet. Then, after Jesus was dead, He come to John the Baptist in a dream and let John know that John had to take over the writin' of the rest of the Bible 'cause Jesus had only three days to work on His resurrection. Both Jesus and John knowed that Jesus's resurrection was gonna be a powerful big deal and would cause a lot of talk, gossip, and general commotion amongst the people wunst the word got out to ever'body that Jesus was alive again and back in town. You know how gossipy people is nowadays, and I reckon they was the same back then. A dead man come back to life is bound to put any gossip's mouth and tongue in high gear. Even as people was gossipin', ole John the Baptist was writin' in the Good Book."

"So you're saying that John the Baptist continued writing the Bible after Jesus's death and resurrection. Hmm ... Just out of curiosity, Country, can you tell me why my Bible at home is called the 'King James Version'?" I asked.

"Yes, I can, but I think that ever'body should thank the Lord that we had John the Baptist who, all by hisself, finished writin' up the rest of the New Testerment. After John the Baptist finished his writin', he handed his work over to King James of England, who was goin' to print up both the Old and New Testerments in the Bible and then commence sellin' the Good Book. Ole King James figgered that the Bible would be a number one bestseller and a real money-maker. So King James commenced to printin' Bibles, and then about a month later, he had more than a million Bibles printed up and stacked up all 'round his castle. Since King James had all the Bibles printed up and ready for sale, folks called them Bibles the 'King James Version Bible.' Mister Ross said the Bible sold out the first day it was up for sale. Bibles was like telervisions—ever'body wanted one. King James charged ever'body two dollars each for a Bible. Ole King James, bless his heart, raked in so much money sellin' them Bibles that he never had to work another day in his life. That's what my Sunday school teacher, Mister Ross, told me."

"What did John the Baptist do after the Bible was published?" I asked.

"Well, John the Baptist went back to baptizin' people like he was fightin' fire. I reckon he was fightin' fire—hellfire, that is. Man, woman, or child, it didn't matter to John. He just throwed people in the water, scrubbed them real good, prayed over 'em, and pitched 'em back on solid ground. Then John would holler, 'Next!' and a brand-new sinner would be dragged into the water. On a good mornin', John could baptize thirty or forty people 'fore dinnertime. Sadly, John was decrapitated by King Herod 'cause he wouldn't dance with the king's daughter, Salami, at her high school prom."

"While he was alive, you could never call John the Baptist a lazy man," I said.

"If they ever was a worker, John the Baptist was one. He worked hard, he preached hard, and he baptized hard. Lots of people don't even know 'bout Jesus and

John the Baptist writin' the King James Bible in what little spare time they had," said Country Jones.

"I, for one, did not know that … uh, that fact," I said. I felt as though I was receiving a theological lesson I would not soon forget.

"You would have knowed all 'bout Jesus and His buddy John the Baptist if Deacon Garland Kyle Ross had been your Sunday school teacher as you growed up, like he was mine. Lord, I wish that ever'body coulda had a Sunday school teacher like Mister Ross. I truly believe our world would be a better place today."

Country Jones bent over and picked up a golf-ball-sized rock, which he threw at a squirrel in a nearby tree. He barely missed, and the tree dweller chattered angrily. Then Country Jones turned back to me. His face became solemn as he began asking me a series of Bible questions.

"Hal, do you know who fit the battle of Jericho?" he asked.

"Joshua," I said confidently.

"I bet you don't know what happened to the walls of Jericho, do you?"

"The walls came tumbling down," I said.

"Who was pestered with boils, sores, and poison oak blisters all over his body, and no matter which way he turned, he run into awful bad luck?"

"I'm gonna make a guess and say Job," I said.

"In the Bible, what color was Joseph's Sunday-go-to-meetin' coat?" asked Country.

"There were many colors in Joseph's coat."

"Well you have had some church-raisin' and Bible-trainin' as you passed through Sunday school. Where do you go to church, Hal?"

"When I go to church, I go to the Healing Waters Baptist Church. I used to go to Brier Creek Baptist Church, but now I go to Healing Waters. The preacher at Brier Creek, Rufus Calloway, died, so my grandparents switched churches. Also, Healing Waters Baptist Church is closer to our house."

"I knowed that man, Preacher Rufus Calloway 'fore he died. I've heard him preach. I liked the way he preached. He could make you feel the fires of hell burnin' your backside right through the wooden pew! Didn't he pass away sudden-like durin' a baptizin'?"

"Yep," I said. Preacher Calloway and his wife had been to my grandpa's house for Sunday dinner several times. I knew him and the story of his death. "Preacher Calloway was baptizing a woman from West Jefferson in the New River when the preacher stepped on a slippery rock under the water. He lost his footing and kept stepping on submerged, slick stones. The preacher fell backwards into deeper, swifter water, probably where a deep hole had washed out during the New River's spring floods. He waved his arms and splashed in the water, but the minister couldn't swim. The New River just swallowed him up. The drowning happened in the afternoon, and his body wasn't found until a week later under a low-water bridge. Fish had nibbled some of his facial flesh away. The woman that Reverend Calloway was trying to baptize could swim, and she made it to shore safely."

"I remember that story, Hal, 'cause the woman, Marsha Clementine Waters, had to get baptized all over again with another preacher, of course," said Country Jones. "I think she was baptized in the waters of Big Horse Creek. The news about Preacher Calloway's passin' hit my Sunday school teacher, Mister Ross, awful hard. He cried when he told our Sunday school class 'bout Preacher Rufus Calloway's passin'. Mister Ross was good friends with the drownded preacher. He said that the preacher's corpse had a big grin on what was left of its face. The searchers found the body bobbin' up and down under that low-water bridge over near Crumpler, just above Riverbend Store. Mister Ross took some comfort in hearin' 'bout that dead preacher's smile. I hope that when I die, I'll have a smile on my face just like Preacher Calloway. Mister Ross says when he dies, he'll have a big grin on his face 'cause he'll be headin' for Glory. He said the first thing he would do in Glory would be to thank Jesus and John the Baptist for writin' the Bible! The next thing he wanted to do was try to find ole King James and shake his hand."

"This Mister Ross of yours must've been an interesting Sunday school teacher. My Sunday school teachers in both churches, Brier Creek and Healing Waters, must've been misinformed because I never heard anything about Jesus or John the Baptist writing parts of the Bible. Your Mister Ross must've been a thought-provoking Sunday school teacher."

"You bet he was! Mister Ross could provoke the dickens out of any thought you might have—or any Sunday school lesson he might teach. That ole Sunday school teacher could make the Bible come alive in his Sunday school classes. Mister Ross always begun Sunday school class by tellin' us kids a little joke, like which is faster, heat or cold? The answer is heat 'cause anybody can catch a cold. Heh! Heh! Sometimes he would give us a problem question to think about, like who crossed the road first, the chicken or the egg? Mister Ross never told us the answer to that one, and I ain't figgered it out yet. I don't know how he done all he done 'cause he couldn't read good."

"Couldn't read?"

"Not good. Mister Ross could read a little, but he never had much schoolin'. He told us in Sunday school class one Sunday mornin' that he never had read the Bible all the way through 'cause readin' give him a fearsome headache after about five minutes of it. He said he had learnt a great deal about the Bible by listenin' to radio preachers, like Billy Sunday, Percy Crawford, and Aimee Semple McPherson amongst others. Mister Ross said he liked old-timey preachin' best if it was fast and loud. That's the way I like my preachin' too."

"I prefer calmer sermons, but tell me more about Mister Ross."

"Mister Ross was borned very young, but when he reached his middle teenage years, on Sunday nights and sometimes on Wednesday nights, he would listen to one radio preacher's message till he got tard of that partic'lar preacher. Then he would twist the radio dial and tune in another radio preacher for a while. Sometimes, Mister Ross turned down the radio and took a nap in between the radio preachers. He said that ever' now and then, his ears would need a rest. Whilst he was sleepin', his daddy would come in and change the channels on the radio. His daddy liked radio preachin' too."

"I can sympathize with the teenaged Mister Ross because I know exactly how he felt. I get sleepy during long sermons," I said, reflecting on lengthy Baptist church sermons. More than once, Grandma Grayson had elbowed me to wake me up during a mid-sermon siesta.

"While he was changin' channels on his radio, once in a while, Mister Ross hit on the Grand Ole Opry station, WSM radio," said Country Jones. "Mister Ross would listen to the Opry for a little while, 'specially if one of the singers was singin' a hymn. He liked that Roy Acuff feller and Little Jimmy Dickens. Mister Ross knowed all the words to 'Betsy the Heifer' and 'Out Behind the Barn.' Both of them songs was sung by Little Jimmy Dickens, who was only a four-foot-tall feller, accordin' to Mister Ross.

"Mister Ross liked the singin' on the grand old Opry, but mostly he liked radio preachin'. On some Sunday nights, Mister Ross said that he would listen to upwards of seven or eight preachers, all of 'em talkin' about diff'rent parts of the Bible. His fav'rite radio preacher was Backwoods Sam Battle. He said that Preacher Battle could preach about hell over the radio and make the hellfire and brimstone so hot that it would singe your eyebrows, kindly like Preacher Rufus Calloway would preach when he was alive."

"Yes, I've had my eyebrows singed a time or two from listening to the late Preacher Rufus Calloway's sermons."

"Mister Ross would sometimes fall asleep late at night, listenin' to them radio preachers, first one follered by another. He'd wake up in the mornin', turn off his radio, and remember 'most ever' word that those preachers had said while he was asleep. I reckon that's how he learnt the Bible so good, Hal."

"I reckon," I mumbled. I was beginning to understand why Country Jones, through the teachings of Mister Ross, had his Bible stories and characters so thoroughly muddled and mixed up.

"Mister Ross is gettin' up in years now, but he still teaches the youth group's Sunday school class at our church. He ain't my Sunday school teacher no more 'cause I have done graduated to the young adult class. I got a big surprise last Sunday when I walked past Mister Ross's youth group Sunday school class. He had a record player goin' and was playin' Wayne Raney's song, 'We Need a Whole Lot More of Jesus and a Lot Less Rock and Roll' for his class. Now there's a song with a real message to it. All the young boys and girls was clappin' their hands and singin' along with Mister Ross and Wayne Raney."

I glanced at my watch. I thrummed my fingers on the Mercury's hood. Patience was not one of my virtues. It was getting late, and I had chores to do before dark.

Country Jones must've noticed my concern because he pointed to his dilapidated truck and said, "Climb in this ole truck, Hal, if you ain't ashamed to be seen in it, and I'll give you a lift home. You live down on the river with your grandmaw and grandpaw, the Graysons, don't you?"

"That's right," I said. "I don't live far from the New River Bridge. I would appreciate a ride, Country. I'll leave my Mercury here in the school's parking lot overnight."

"All right, get in, Hal, and we'll be on our way."

PART 2

I had climbed in the pickup's cab and pushed Country Jones's guitar to the center of the truck's bench seat. Country fastened the guitar securely with a little leather strap from behind the truck's seat. Country turned on the ignition. The pickup coughed like a man with pneumonia, spat like an angry cat, shuddered like a wet dog, and expelled puffs of black smoke like a big-city factory.

"Watch your feet, Hal," Country had warned as I scrambled into his corroded truck. I looked down at what remained of the pickup's floorboard. I could've put my foot through one of the larger holes, and the parking lot gravel beneath the pickup truck was visible. "I've been meanin' to patch up them holes usin' tar, screen-door parts, pole bean sticks, and thick cardboard paper, but I ain't got around to it yet."

Country Jones popped the clutch, and we were off, bouncing through the Central Ashe High School's parking lot and out onto the paved highway. Through a couple of the floorboard holes, I could see the highway pavement and white lines spinning beneath my feet. On the two-lane highway, we soon reached the pickup's maximum speed of forty-five miles per hour. I lifted my tennis-shoe clad feet and placed them on the dashboard. I was careful not to disturb the plastic Jesus mounted on the dash, just above the radio. The pickup's seat felt surprisingly comfortable. I settled back, determined to enjoy the ride home.

The pickup's radio was functional, and we listened to George Jones's version of "White Lightnin'" as we rode past houses, fields, and farms. Country Jones turned the volume up and sang along with George Jones, never missing a beat or a lyric. He drove with one hand and slapped his thigh with the other in perfect rhythm to the fast-moving tune about owning stills and moonshining in the hills of North Carolina. The song ended and the radio station began a commercial. Country turned the radio's volume down. "George Jones is my fav'rite livin' country singer. What a pure country voice that George Jones has got!" he explained as the pickup clattered over a pothole. One of the front tires developed a whine.

"I like George Jones too. Who is your favorite dead country singer?" I asked, somewhat interested but mostly making conversation.

"Hank Williams, of course. Ain't he ever'body's fav'rite dead country singer?" Country Jones eyed me curiously, as if he were having doubts about my intelligence, not to mention my taste in music. The old pickup growled when he shifted into a lower gear as we climbed a hill.

"I don't know. I guess I don't think much about dead country singers," I replied. "What if something happened to George Jones and he passed away? Who would be your favorite dead country singer then, George Jones or Hank Williams?"

"I reckon I'd have to stick with Hank Williams," said Country. "What I like about ole Hank is that he mostly wrote his own songs, and them songs was gen'rally 'bout bein' lonesome and blue, and sometimes 'bout bein' in love with a cheatin' woman, and other times 'bout bein' happy-go-lucky and free, but mostly Hank's songs was 'bout bein' lonesome and blue. He died in the backseat of a Cadillac on January 1, 1953. Ole Hank was only twenty-nine years of age when he died."

Country's guitar, resting between us, shifted slightly as we rounded a curve. "How long have you had this guitar, Country?"

"My daddy give me that guitar for Christmas when I was ten years old, and by the time I was eleven, I could play that guitar purty good. And besides givin' me the guitar, Daddy Jones said that ten years old was old enough to stay up and listen to the Grand Ole Opry. Like Mister Ross, I loved Roy Acuff on the Grand Ole Opry. It wasn't long till I learnt all the words to the 'Wabash Cannonball.' I've been playin' the guitar and makin' up songs since my tenth birthday. By the time I was twelve, I could play 'The Wildwood Flower' so that you could recognize it. I'm a better picker now than I was back then."

"I've heard you play your guitar and sing in the school cafeteria before first period classes. You're pretty good."

Country Jones was not quite ready for Nashville, but I told the truth when I said he was good, especially for his age.

"Daddy Jones wunst told me, 'If you want to learn about country music, listen to ole Hank Williams. He can make folks laugh or make 'em cry.' Yessir, that's what my daddy said about Hank Williams. Lemme see if I can find a good station. They play Hank Williams music all the time on the radio now."

Country began twisting the dials of the radio, trying in vain to tune in a country station playing a Hank Williams song. We crested the hill, and I could see the bluish-green waters of the winding New River in the distance. Country Jones applied the brakes, and the rusty old truck slowed down. He looked not at the road but at his radio dial as the pickup creeped along.

"I can't find no Hank Williams music, but here's a Hank you might like—Hank Snow." His callused farm-boy fingers precision tuned the dial.

Hank Snow, backed up by guitars and a fiddle, sang about a train, an unfaithful girlfriend, and his need to keep "movin' on." Hank Snow's voice was deep, nasal, and distinctive, like the voice of a younger country singer named Johnny Cash. I took the liberty of turning the radio up. Country Jones grinned and pressed the accelerator. The pickup chugged forward.

"Right after this message, we'll hear a song by Hank Thompson," announced the country disc jockey. The radio message was an ad pointing out that it was impossible to make good biscuits without Martha White Self-Rising Flour. After the advertisement, the sounds of guitars and Hank Thompson's pleasant nasal twang filled the pickup's cabin. Thompson's song, "The Wild Side of Life," was about honky-tonk angels, one in particular, who seemed to be enjoying the wild side of life. Hank Thompson, or his songwriter, seemed upset that any married woman might leave a marriage and spend her time at the honky-tonk bars. Country Jones informed me that a female singer named Kitty Wells had recorded a response to Hank Thompson's honky-tonk song. All the women folks, according to Country, liked Kitty Wells' answer song. The song was called "It Wasn't God Who Made Honky-Tonk Angels."

"Them two songs was pop'lar back in the early fifties," Country said. "The country disc jockeys would play Hank Thompson's song and Kitty Wells' answer song back-to-back, you know. Them two songs sold a mess of records and made a lot of money for Kitty Wells and Hank Thompson."

"There sure are lots of famous country singers named 'Hank,'" I said when "The Wild Side of Life" ended. We came to a straight stretch in the road, and Country accelerated. I glanced at the speedometer. We were going thirty-five miles per hour.

"Yeah, there's Hank Snow, Hank Locklin, Hank Thompson, and the late, great Hank Williams. That's what they say on the radio 'fore they play one of Hank's songs. 'Here's the late, great Hank Williams to sing one of his songs.' Let's see now, I named Snow, Locklin, Thompson, and Williams. All of 'em Hanks. That's all the Hanks I can think of right off the top of my head, and that's only four Hanks. I reckon there's room for a few more men named 'Hank' in country music. I have heard that Hank Williams had a son, and that his name is Hank Williams, Junior. I wish that little young'un all the luck in the world. Growin' up without a daddy is gotta be hard enough, let alone growin' up without his famous daddy. I bet that little feller will spend a lot of hours askin' questions 'bout his daddy, Hank Williams, and listenin' to his daddy's old records. I'm glad my daddy ain't famous like Hank Williams was. Daddy Jones ain't very well-knowed outside of the holler where we live. That suits him just fine. He don't want to be famous, but sometimes I wonder what it would be like to be famous. Don't you, Hal?"

"Famous like Elvis Presley?"

"No, famous like Hank Williams," said Country Jones.

Country slowed his truck as he saw a stooped old lady, cane in hand, standing beside a rusty mailbox and reading her mail. She had on an oversized straw hat and a white shawl over a tattered pink bathrobe. She wore floppy white bedroom slippers. She stood with one of her slippers on the asphalt highway. She seemed oblivious to any traffic that might pass her way.

Country brought his pickup to a stop. "Howdy, Mrs. Russell! How you doin' today?"

"Country Jones, you'd better slow that vehicle of yours down! I seen you racin' your truck down this highway early this mornin'. You're gonna run over and kill somebody one of these days. Next time I see him, I'll tell your daddy that you've been speedin' up and down this highway like a juvenile delinquent. Mark my words, young man, you'll end up in jail one of these days."

"Don't worry, ma'am, I'll be real careful. Tell Mister Russell I said 'howdy,'" declared Country. He whispered, "Mrs. Russell likes to fuss, but she's got a good heart. She won't tell Daddy Jones nothin'."

He maneuvered the pickup safely around the elderly woman. Then, shifting gears, he picked up speed. The pickup swerved around a few curves as we reached the top of a hill. Country Jones let the pickup coast down the hill toward the New River. I pointed out the dirt road that led to my house in plenty of time for him to turn right. He turned, leaving the paved road. A 1955 Chevrolet Bel-Air ahead of us left a trail of dust drifting through the air. Country drove through the earthbound cloud, leaving his clean windshield covered with a thin layer of dust.

"My mama and daddy almost changed my name to 'Hank' after Hank Williams, but they kept my name as Country. My middle name is 'Sammy' 'cause Mama named me after her little brother who had died of the brain fever when he was only six years old. Little Sammy woke up with a bad headache and by nightfall he was dead. We only got two faded pictures of Sammy. In one, he is settin' in a toy wagon. In the other, Sammy's got his arms around a big ole collie dog. My full name is 'Country Sammy Bliss Sunset Butterfly Sweetpea Roosevelt Jones.' You see, Hal, my mama and daddy let each of my five older sisters give me one name apiece. On my birth certificate, though, it just says 'Country Sammy Jones.'"

"Wow! Your older sisters must've had fun naming you. They came up with some creative names."

"Yep, but the one who had the most fun was my youngest older sister. She give me the name 'Butterfly.' Mama said she wouldn't call me nothin' but Butterfly up till the time I started walkin'. My mama told me that I growed so fast that it wasn't no time till I was just as tall as my youngest older sister. Mama said I made her quit callin' me 'Butterfly' as soon as I got to be as big as she was."

"What's her name?" I asked.

"Do you mean my mama's name or my youngest older sister's name?"

"Your youngest older sister's name."

"Crystal Lynn Heaven Mockin'bird Christmas Strawberry Jones," replied Country Jones. "All my sisters is purty, but I reckon that she is the purtiest one. She's got natural curly yeller hair and sky-blue eyes. Crystal Lynn Heaven Mockin'bird Christmas Strawberry Jones is married now and expectin' her first young'un in a month or two. Since she's married, her full name now is 'Crystal Lynn Heaven Mockin'bird Christmas Strawberry Jones Blevins.'"

"What's her husband's name?"

"Al."

"Al?"

"Al Blevins, but most folks calls him 'Shorty' Blevins. He's just a smidgen over five foot tall. Shorty was raised over in the Clifton Township."

Suddenly, Country Jones slammed on the brakes. The tires screeched, and the pickup skidded to a stop. I lurched toward the windshield, but I caught myself by throwing my hands forward onto the pickup's dashboard and bracing myself. A fog made of dust surrounded the truck.

"Hey, ain't that a white-tailed deer out there in the middle of the river? Look over yonder by that big rock!"

He pointed a tanned finger—dotted with freckles—and I looked out through the dusty windshield. Sure enough, a doe, midstream in the New River, was drinking. The soft-eyed doe, knee-deep in river water, lifted her head, waved her long ears, and sniffed the air. Country Jones stepped on the gas pedal, and as the pickup rattled forward, the startled deer bounded toward the far shore, flashing her white tail and splashing jeweled droplets of water along her sides. Reaching the shore, the doe leaped over a split-rail fence and vanished into the trees that lined the New River's far bank.

"There ain't no critter on God's green earth that is more graceful than what a deer is. I love to see 'em run and jump over fences. Don't you, Hal?"

I nodded in the affirmative. Just then, we hit a deep pothole in the road. The bone-jarring impact caused the pickup's hood to fly upward about a foot until it was caught by a homemade restraining device made mostly of chicken wire. With a whump, the hood fell solidly back into place. I looked out upon the pickup's rusty hood and saw what appeared to be a bullet hole. I asked Country if it really was a bullet hole.

He laughed and slapped his knee. "Yep, Daddy Jones made that bullet hole a while back 'fore I got my driver's license. The pickup wouldn't start one mornin', and

Daddy got madder and madder 'cause he was runnin' late for a meetin'. Ever'time Daddy Jones tried to crank the truck, the engine would sound like it was gonna start, but then the motor would die. Daddy was supposed to meet Shade Barlow that mornin'. I reckon he was goin' to pick up some moonshine whiskey, but, try as Daddy might, the ole truck's motor wouldn't turn over. Lord, he got his dander up that mornin'. He begun to cuss the truck and kick at the fenders and tires. Why, he even put his fist through the passenger side winder, bustin' the glass out and slingin' shards ever'wheres. Fin'ly, Daddy Jones went fussin' and fumin' into the house and come out with his ole army pistol. He slammed the screen door real hard, and Rustybutt, our ole beagle, come runnin' out from under the porch, barkin' his fool head off.

"Mama Jones stood in the doorway and hollered, 'Fonzie, put that pistol down and come back in here and finish your breakfast! These here biscuits is already so cold, they won't melt butter.'

"Daddy paid Mama no mind. He stomped down the front porch steps, raised his pistol, and took aim at the pickup truck. He was so mad that his hand was a-shakin'. He shot the pickup once in the hood over the motor, but the bullet didn't hit no vital engine parts. When Daddy tried to shoot the gun again, the revolver just clicked 'cause he hadn't put but one bullet in the chamber the last time he loaded it. He throwed the gun down and begun to cuss the pistol and then begun to kick the gun all around the yard. But Daddy only *thought* he had put one bullet in that gun. Daddy was wrong. Dead wrong."

"You mean the gun was still loaded?"

"That's right, Hal. When Daddy Jones drinks too much, he gets right forgetful. I reckon he was drinkin' when he loaded his pistol. On the fourth kick from Daddy's brogan, the revolver fired—*Bang!*—and the weapon flew backards 'bout a foot. It was a wonder one of us Joneses hadn't been shot and maybe kilt 'cause all us Jones young'uns, along with Mama, had gathered 'round the pickup truck, laughin' and pointin' fingers at Daddy. We was all makin' fun of him when his gun went off—*Kapow!*—and Mama screamed loud as a panther and sprung up 'bout a foot in the air. My heart jumped and thumped in my chest. My youngest older sister, Crystal Lynn Heaven Mockin'bird Christmas Strawberry Jones, wet her drawers and run back into the house to change. All of us Joneses was shocked and shakin', includin' Daddy Jones. Thank goodness, nobody in the fam'ly was hurt by the bullet fired from the pistol gun. The good Lord must've been lookin' out for us Joneses. Praise to the Almighty that no harm nor no damage was done to us when that pistol went off right there in the yard with us Joneses crowded around in a circle, laughin' at Daddy."

"Thank goodness nobody was hurt."

"Kilt a chicken."

"Killed a what?" I asked.

"One of our chickens, Hal. The bullet went right through the chicken's gizzard, killin' it straightaway. A chicken can't live but a few seconds without a gizzard to digest the ox'gen in the air and push out the carbon peroxide from its body. The shot chicken fell over, and though the chicken was stone dead with her eyes already glazed over, the Dominecker hen got up on her feet and scuttled around the yard sev'ral times, feathers flyin' ever' whichaway. That ain't nothin' 'cause I've seen many a kilt chicken run like that after Daddy chopped their heads clean off."

"I've seen chickens do that too," I said.

"Granny Jones don't even bother with a hatchet. She just wrings a chicken's neck by spinnin' a chicken's body 'round whilst she grips it by the head and beak. Granny Jones ends up with the chicken's head in her hand whilst the carcass hits the ground, pops up, and takes off runnin'. Headless chickens don't run far, but they do run right fast. Granny Jones said that the faster a chicken runs after it dies, the more tender the breast meat will be. She gen'rally throwed the chicken heads in the river to get shed of 'em. She called chicken heads 'fish food.' Granny Jones can still heave a chicken head pert near as far as I can throw a baseball.

"But that partic'lar chicken, the little Dominecker, which Daddy shot, run faster and futher than any dead chicken I ever seen. It was lucky for us that hen—Mama Jones had named her 'Minerva'—run 'round in circles and stayed purty close to where she was kilt, or the chicken would've run all the way across our yard and into the deep woods."

"Minerva?"

"Yeah, I hated that it was Minerva which got kilt 'cause she never caused no harm on the farm, sorta kept to herself. She was always a friendly chicken, and she laid the best tastin' little brown eggs. Minerva never complained, neither. You seldom heard a peep outta her.

If there's a Heaven for chickens, that little Dominecker hen is prob'ly lookin' down on us now, cluckin' for joy and peckin' at solid gold corn spread out all over Glory Land. Yessir, Minerva was a awful good hen, and her dyin' come so sudden-like. There was no way my fam'ly could prepare theirselves for Minerva's hasty passin'."

Driving with one hand, Country Jones pulled a bandanna from his hip pocket and wiped his moistening eyes. He snuffled and blew his nose, then placed the bandanna back in his hip pocket. Country Jones gave me a sheepish smile.

"Are you all right, Country?" I asked. "Shouldn't you keep both hands on the steering wheel?"

"You got to excuse me, Hal. I'm awful tenderhearted. Just thinkin' about Minerva's passin' causes me to tear up a little. I'm softhearted like my daddy. I take after him, I reckon. After three or four drinks of moonshine and with a few Hank Williams songs playin' on the radio, Daddy Jones will start blubberin' for no reason at all, hardly. When he said grace at suppertime on the afternoon of the accidental chicken-shootin', Daddy Jones throwed in some awful nice words about the late hen, Minerva, 'fore we commenced eatin' her. She fried up real tender and tasted mighty good. I doubt if we Joneses will ever have another chicken like Minerva on our farm. Chickens like her only come along wunst in a lifetime."

Country Jones sighed and stared straight ahead as the pickup rattled and bounced along the road. His lower lip quivered.

"I'm sorry that you lost Minerva. She must've been quite a chicken," I said.

"She was. On the other hand, Hal, we got a little banty rooster named 'Caliban' that has the full-sized roosters scared of him. That little sumbitch, Caliban, is the most vicious, bloodthirsty chicken I ever seen. Caliban don't like people, nor dogs, nor other roosters, nor nothin' 'cept for hens. Boy, does that pint-sized rooster like big ole hens. Caliban chases after 'em from dawn to dusk. He also likes to pester people who come around the chicken houses."

"What does he do to bother people?"

"Caliban will sneak up behind a person, peck him on the ankle or shin hard enough to bring the blood, and then take off runnin' so fast that no human bean couldn't never catch him."

"Can banty roosters mate with the larger hens?" I asked. The question had never come up in biology class at Central Ashe High School.

"I don't know if Caliban can accomplish anythin', but he tries like the devil to breed with our full-size hens. Daddy Jones calls Caliban 'a horny little bastard.' I don't know if Caliban can mate with them big chickens 'cause those hens is so much bigger and longer-legged than what he is, but I do know that, lately, we've had some scrawny, undersized pullets on the farm. I think Caliban is the daddy of them runty chickens, but Daddy Jones don't think so. Daddy thinks most of the big, long-legged woman chickens could outrun Caliban. Daddy says the runt pullets is due to a bad batch of chicken feed we got at Brown's Hardware and Feed Store. We fed that sorry chicken feed to them pullets when they was little baby chicks. Daddy stays away from the brand called 'Red Barn Chick Starter Feed.' He always buys 'Backyard Rooster and Hen Feed' nowadays."

"That's the brand my grandpa feeds our chickens."

Country Jones nodded his head and grinned. "Daddy Jones vows that he will wring Caliban's neck one of these days, but Daddy can't catch him. Even us kids can't run that rooster down. And Daddy Jones says Caliban ain't worth the cost of a bullet. When Caliban dies, most likely of old age, I reckon he'll bust chicken hell wide open, if they is a chicken Hades. Here on Earth, that Caliban has been one ornery little rooster. I wonder why Minerva died so sudden-like and Caliban lives on and on. It's a mystery to me."

"That's a theological question. You might want to ask your former Sunday school teacher, Mister Ross, about blameless Aphrodite's short life, and Caliban's long sporting life spent, for the most part, chasing long-legged hens."

"That's a good idee. I'll ask Mister Ross this comin' Sunday if I don't see him sooner."

"Go on with your story about the bullet hole in this old truck, Country."

"Well, when the ruckus involvin' this ole pickup, the gun, and the dead chicken was over with, Daddy Jones sighed, dabbed his eyeballs with a handkerchief, and walked real slow back to the house. His shoulders was stooped over, and his head was leanin' forward like he was real tard. Mama Jones follered Daddy, who was carryin' his pistol real careful-like. Daddy stopped just long enough to squat down and pick up the shot chicken. He stuck the pistol in his pants pocket and started pluckin' Minerva's feathers as he made his way up the porch steps. He laid the chicken's carcass on the top porch step and went inside the house. Mama Jones follered Daddy through the screen door. I could hear him fussin' and frettin' inside the parlor. Then he got real mad and started throwing things 'round inside the house. Daddy broke one antique chair that used to belong to his great grandma. I heard Mama holler, 'Put that lamp down, Fonzie Jones, or you'll be sleepin' in the barn tonight!'

"Then Daddy switched gears and got to cussin' the gov'ment for some reason. Mainly, he cussed the gov'ment in Warshington DC, but he didn't leave out the state gov'ment down yonder in Raleigh neither. He begun by cussin' the Democrats for a while and then he would cuss the Republicans.

"Mama has said to me, 'Don't never try to reason with Fonzie when he's cussin' the gov'ment. It can't be done. He won't listen to reason. For the life of me, I don't see why Fonzie gets so all fired up about the gov'ment. He ain't even registered to vote.' One thing's for sure, Hal, the whole Jones family has learnt to stay away from Daddy Jones when he starts in on the gov'ment.

"It was not long after that accidental chicken-shootin' that Daddy give me this here ole pickup truck. Daddy said, 'Country, this rattletrap of a truck ain't brought me nothin' but bad luck. Maybe you'll have better luck with the vehicle than what I did.'

"I patched the ole truck up as best I could, put in a new bat'ry, a new set of spark plugs, and got her runnin' again. I named her 'Nellybelle,' and I change her oil reg'lar. She needs new tars, but I can't afford 'em. I can't even afford recaps."

"Don't feel like the Lone Ranger," I said, making Country Jones grin.

Nellybelle rumbled along, kicking up dust. Country Jones patted the old truck's dashboard and said, "She's a purty good ole truck. She ain't never left me stranded on the side of the road. Not never."

"I'll be getting out at the next house, Country." I pointed to my grandfather's white frame house, which overlooked the New River. The pickup juddered over the low-water bridge. A startled bullfrog splashed into the water. "Just turn in here, Country," I said. "Thanks for the ride."

Country pumped the brakes a few times and the pickup stopped with a squeal. The truck's engine, still running, clattered, knocked, and whined. I got out and reminded Country about the jumper cables. I held the truck's door open so I could hear what Country said.

"Hal, I'll bring my daddy's jumper cables to school tomorrow. We'll get your Mercury started up in no time."

"Thanks, Country," I said. I closed the pickup's door carefully, lest it fall off in the Grayson's gravel driveway.

Country Jones smiled and waved goodbye. The pickup growled and sprang forward. Country and Nellybelle disappeared, rattling away in a cloud of dust and blue smoke.

I rode school bus number 29 to Central Ashe High School the next day, and, true to his word, Country Jones brought his father's jumper cables. After school, he pulled his old truck up to the front end of my Mercury. We hooked the jumper cables to the batteries of both vehicles. Country and I managed to get my Mercury started fifteen minutes after school had been dismissed. My car's engine ran smoothly.

"Well, let's see …" Country Jones said, his hand on the Mercury's roof as he talked to me through the open driver-side window. I sat behind the steering wheel, adjusting the rearview mirror to my satisfaction. When the mirror's adjustment was complete, I gave Country Jones my full attention.

"Today's Friday, Hal, and you told me that you got a date with that purty Miss Sophie Bishop tonight. I think your Mercury's bat'ry will be all right, but be sure to stop at that Esso service station at the foot of the hill and have somebody there check your bat'ry. If they say it's all right, which I figger they will, then you might want to drive 'round a little while to charge it up."

"I'll stop at the gas station and have the mechanic check out the battery. The drive home should charge it."

"Yep, that should do it. One more thing, Hal, and this is 'bout your girlfriend, not your Mercury. My daddy seen Miss Sophie at church a few Sundays ago, and Daddy Jones talked 'bout how purty she was. It was at dinnertime, and he said, and these is his exact words, 'That Bishop gal looks like a movie star with them green eyes and all that wavy black hair. Her figger ain't bad neither. She's all growed up now and purty as a picture!' Daddy went on and on about your Miss Sophie till it pissed off Mama Jones. I thought they was goin' to have one of their spats, but our whole family was settin' around the Sunday dinner table, and Grandpa Jones begun sayin' grace real loud. That quieted the both of 'em down. By the time Grandpa finished sayin' grace, and we all had said, 'Amen,' things was peaceful around the table."

"Thanks for your help, Country, in getting this old car started," I said. "I'll see you at school on Monday. Now, I have to get on home, do a few chores, and then get cleaned up for my date with Sophia."

"I know what you're talkin' 'bout, Hal. I've got a date with Maude Pugh on Saturday. Her daddy must be rich 'cause they've got a television set. It's black 'n white, but the picture is just as plain as it can be, no snow to speak of. That little TV set can pick up three channels, and I reckon that's all folks would ever need. Maude's mama and daddy is goin' to the races in Wilkesboro town on Saturday night. They're takin' Maude's oldest brother, Durwood, with 'em. Maude and me is just goin' to stay at her house and pop some corn and set 'round and watch television. We got to babysit her littlest brother Mack, but he gets sleepy real early. I'm takin' my guitar, just in case she wants to hear a little music. Well, so long, and tell Miss Sophie that I said 'howdy' and give her a big ole birthday kiss for me!"

"I plan to do just that, Country," I said.

"Speakin' of kissin', my Maude is missin' her two front teeth, which makes for some interestin' romantical slobber-swappin', let me tell you! Lord have mercy on us all, can that gal kiss! Whee doggies! Well, so long, Hal, and don't you dare forget to tell Miss Sophie that I said 'howdy' and tell her I wish her a happy birthday with many more to come."

"I'll do that," I promised. I put my Mercury in drive and headed for the Jefferson Esso station, which was only a short distance away. After driving a mile or two, I saw Country Jones's truck appear in my rearview mirror. I was sure Country was following me to make sure my Mercury and I made it safely to the Esso station.

* * *

At Central Ashe High School, I had four friends I could count on because they had proven their loyalty over the years. One was big Tank Banner, the strongest teenager in the county. Another was redheaded, freckle-faced Pudge Hawkins, who had been my friend forever it seemed. Pudge and I had become friends before we entered first grade at Healing Waters Elementary School. The other two were John Bowman, who was said to be the most intelligent student at Central Ashe and perhaps the smartest young man in the county, and Gene Clodfelter, who had earned the reputation of being the meanest—I should say "most mischievous or orneriest"—kid in school. Of course, I had other friends, but Tank, Pudge, John, and Gene were my *best* friends. I now decided to add another best friend: Country Jones.

Country Jones had stopped to help me as I stood alone in the Central Ashe parking lot beside my stalled Mercury. He shared with me some of his religious beliefs. When Country decided my Mercury's battery was dead, he'd given me a ride home in his old pickup. I'd seen Country in the high school halls, but I'd never gotten to know him. I'd never talked with him for more than a minute or two. On the drive to my home, he told me about members of his family and his girlfriend Maude. I learned that he loved country music, especially the music of Hank Williams. The next day, Country had brought his father's jumper cables to get my car started. He followed me to the local Esso station to make sure I didn't have any more car trouble on the way. He reminded me of the biblical Good Samaritan. His "mountain talk," or his "Appalachian dialect," was as agreeable to me as a dipper of cool spring water on a hot day.

In English class on the Monday after Country Jones had "rescued" my lifeless Mercury, Mr. Dickinson initiated a class discussion about friendship. We had read James S. Pooler's short story "Shago," which was about a baseball-playing boy who was slowly going blind. Shago, although losing his ball-playing skills due to poor vision, had kept his circle of young friends. With our literature books closed and our dictionaries under our desks, we were asked to define or discuss the word "friend" or "friendship."

"Let's begin our discussion," said Mr. Dickinson. He shuffled a deck of cards. On the face of each card was the name of a student. He drew two cards from the deck. "The fates have chosen Douglas Banner to start. I'll call on Eugene Clodfelter next. Well, Tank, what are your thoughts on friendship?"

Big Tank Banner said, "Two people who become friends must show each other honesty, loyalty, and understanding. Those are the three qualities I look for in a friend."

Eugene Clifton Clodfelter said a friend was "a feller whose girlfriend you ain't stole away … yet!" Gene was not the only student in the classroom who chuckled.

Pudge Hawkins' comments on friendship included these three words: kindness, compassion, and empathy. "Also, a good sense of humor is important," said Pudge.

Country Jones joined the discussion and said, "Well, findin' a good friend, a true-blue friend, is like tryin' to find a four-leaf clover in a big patch of clover. In all my seventeen years, I have found only two four-leaf clovers. Folks says that if you do find a four-leaf clover, it'll bring you good luck. In 'Shago,' the boy goin' blind was real lucky to have such good friends. They let him pitch as long as he could, and then they let him play in the outfield for as long as he could. They was friendly to him even when he couldn't play ball no more 'cause of his blindness. Reminds me of what Granddaddy Jones says 'bout friendship, 'A friend in need is a friend indeed.' I reckon that sayin' means you ort to help out any friend that gets in trouble. Anyways, findin' a real good friend is a whole lot better than findin' a four-leaf clover 'cause its luck lasts only 'bout a week—two weeks at the most. But a friendship might last for a lifetime. My daddy has sev'ral longtime friends. One of 'em, Buster Clyde Barton, better knowed as 'Booger' Barton, is real old. Booger is goin' on sixty. I hope the friends I've made here at Central Ashe High School will last me for a lifetime.

Mister Dickinson, I reckon that's all I got to say 'bout friends and friendship."

Afternoon sunlight was filtering through thinning clouds, brightening Mr. Dickinson's classroom as Country Jones concluded his remarks. I was sitting three desks behind him, taking a few notes but mostly doodling on my notebook paper. Country's ears had turned bright red as soon as he joined the class discussion. I noticed that Tank Banner and Pudge Hawkins, who sat in desks on the classroom's front row, had turned in their desks so they faced Country Jones. They smiled and nodded during Country's comments.

***

On the last day of school, when we were in the third grade at Healing Waters Elementary School, Gene Clodfelter had brought to school a long, sharp needle from his mother's sewing kit. In the boys' restroom after lunch, using the needle, he poked Tank's thumb, bringing forth bright red blood. He jabbed Pudge's thumb and then mine. It hurt but not bad. Then Gene closed his eyes and thrust the needle into his left thumb. We rubbed our bleeding thumbs together, mixing our blood.

"Now the four of us is blood brothers," Gene had said. "That means we gotta look out for one another and be best friends for the rest of our lives. Does ever'body swear to it?"

We swore.

Country Jones and I were not blood brothers like Tank, Pudge, Gene, and me, but as our teenage years passed, Country proved to be a genuine friend. He once said to me, "I ain't gonna have my thumb pricked with no needle nor jabbed with no sharp knife 'cause I can't stand the sight of blood, 'specially my own. But if you're willin', Hal, I reckon we can be brothers without the blood. I ain't got no brothers, just sisters."

"I'm willing, Country. From this moment on, we'll be brothers without the blood. Let's shake on it."

We shook hands. My right hand disappeared into his large calloused palm. We were teenagers back then, and I didn't know our friendship would last a lifetime. It did.

I lost my lifelong friend, my brother without the blood, to a heart attack last week. He died one week after his seventy-fifth birthday.

The last time I saw Country, he was in the Ashe Memorial Hospital having suffered his third heart attack. He lay in a hospital bed on a white sheet and under another white sheet and a light-weight white blanket. His face was creased with deep wrinkles, and his hair, once a deep rusty red, had turned silver. He raised his head from his snow-white pillow and spoke. "Well, if it ain't my ole buddy, Hal Grayson. Ain't you a sight for sore eyes? You done come here to pay your last respects, I reckon."

"No, I came to thank you for your friendship over all these years, and I'm sure you'll be up and around in no time. You'll be going home soon."

"Nope, this time I'm headin' for the last roundup, as the cowboys says in their songs. But I don't mind, not one little bit. I've had a good long life. Maude and me raised two fine sons. One, Halbert, growed up to be a medical doctor and the other, Douglas, a lawyer.

I reckon they got their smarts from Maude's side of the fam'ly. My sons has give me four grandbabies, two boys and two girls. Them little young'uns has lit up my life these past few years. Also, I've made sev'ral good, true-blue friends in my lifetime, like you and Tank Banner and Pudge Hawkins. I ain't got no regrets 'bout leavin' this ole world. I ain't scared. My Baptist faith is as strong as ever, and I know I'll be seein' my Maude, ole Noah, and Jesus up yonder in heaven. I bet Mister Ross, my Sunday school teacher from long ago, will be standin' right there at the pearly gates along with Saint Peter to welcome me."

I pulled a chair up next to Country's bed and sat down. We were two old men reminiscing. We recalled memories of our teenage years, and our vehicles—my old Mercury and his dilapidated, pieced-together truck which was "mostly a Ford." Country remembered the several times he and Maude had double-dated with me and my high school girlfriend, Sophia Bishop. He reminded me that I had served as his best man when he and Maude got married. Country was only twenty years old; his bride, Maude Pugh, was nineteen. "Hal, I reckon you remember that time we had to collect a bunch of money so that we could bail Gene Clodfelter outta jail so's he could get married. Ole Gene, after a night of drinkin' moonshine, woke up in jail on the mornin' of his weddin' day. We bailed him out, dressed him up, and got him to the church on time. When he said, 'I do,' he was still 'bout half drunk."

"I remember," I laughed.

Country laughed along with me, but his laughter was interrupted by a coughing spell. He gasped and placed his right hand on his chest. "Hal, you're gonna have to excuse me. I'm gettin' awful tard and sleepy. I reckon I need some shut-eye."

Country Jones shut his eyes and took a deep breath. His closed lips smiled as he fell into a deep slumber. I got up to leave just as a nurse, followed by a doctor, came into the hospital room. The nurse walked over to Country's bedside, lifted his wrist, and took his pulse. The doctor, using the chest piece of his stethoscope, listened to Country's heartbeat. The doctor frowned.

"He's sleeping," I said. "He told me he was very tired. Try not to wake him."

"I'm sorry, Mister Grayson," said the nurse as she and the doctor pulled part of the bedclothes—a white sheet—up and over Country's face. "Mister Jones is not sleeping."

My lifelong friend, Country Jones, was gone.

TWO LAB PUPPIES

As I looked through the local newspaper, I came across an ad for Labrador retriever puppies. Because of an illness, our veterinarian had euthanized our eight-year-old yellow Lab, Buttermilk. I called my wife Mary over so she could read the ad. I handed her the newspaper's advertisement section. Her eyes scanned the page.

Beautiful blonde Lab puppies for sale. Born April 22. Wormed and ready to go! Both mother and father on premises. Eight puppies, four males and four females. $100 each.

"That's a great price for a purebred Lab pup. Write down the telephone number, and I'll call and get directions," said Mary. "I'd like to see those pups."

***

The next day, with one hundred fifty dollars in my wallet, I drove our Subaru around winding Watauga County roads. Finally, after a steep climb on a dirt road, Mary and I saw a sign reading, *Mountaintop Farm.* We pulled into a gravel driveway in front of a neat, brick farmhouse. Several dogs of various breeds barked their greetings. Among the barking adult dogs, we saw four dogs that were purebred Labs. One Labrador retriever with swollen teats was obviously the mother of the pups we had come to see.

Mr. Grady Timmons, owner of the North Carolina farm, descended his porch steps. He was dressed in a faded blue flannel shirt and bib overalls. He was tall, well over six feet, and lanky. His hair was black with streaks of gray; his face and hands were rough and red. "Howdy, folks. I reckon you're here to look at the pups."

We were taken to an enclosure that contained eight yellow Labrador retriever puppies. They were all healthy and friendly, begging for our attention. They licked our shoes and then our hands when we knelt to pet them. In the avalanche of puppies, I looked around for one that displayed confidence and a good level of activity. One pup in particular held her head high and wagged her tail enthusiastically. She was neither too thin nor too fat. I picked her up, and she relaxed in my arms. She raised her head and looked up at me. The pup had clear brown eyes, and she reacted immediately when my wife snapped her fingers to check the dog's hearing. I cuddled her as she nuzzled and gently nibbled my fingers. The Lab pup and I formed a bond that would last the rest of her life.

Meanwhile, Mary had picked up the fattest puppy in the litter. I was witness to a love at first sight between my wife and that little Lab. The pup squirmed then settled down in Mary's arms. "Can't we get *two* pups?" she asked, holding up the plump female puppy, which was straining to lick her face. "This pup is adorable!"

"We can't afford to buy two pups. You know that," I said.

Mary and I were North Carolina teachers. I taught in Ashe County; Mary taught in Watauga County. During the school year, we had saved enough money to get us through the summer months with no pay. Still, money was tight in our household. Our next checks wouldn't arrive until September.

Unexpectedly, a woman made her way carefully down the brick farmhouse's porch steps. She wore a floral print dress and an apron. Under her left arm was a crutch, and there was also a brace on her left leg. She raised her right hand to shield her eyes from the bright sunlight.

"Grady, give them folks two pups for the price of one!" she called. "We got way too many dogs. Not countin' the pups, I'm feedin' seven dogs. We gotta get shed of some of them puppies as fast as we can. Ain't no way I'm gonna feed nine or ten dogs this winter."

"I reckon you're right, Sadie," said Grady Timmons. "Folks, you can have both of them female puppies that you're holdin' for one hunderd dollars. Is it a deal?"

I pulled a one-hundred-dollar bill from my wallet and then added another twenty. I placed both bills in Grady Timmons' hand.

"That's all I can spare," I said. "I wish I could give you more."

He smiled, stuck the money in his pocket, and shook my hand. "Don't worry 'bout it. I've got a pasteboard box that you can use to carry 'em home in."

He and I put the wriggling puppies into the box. Then he called the mother dog over to say goodbye to her pups. She sniffed and licked her two puppies for the final time, but the Lab mom would not be lonely. She still had six pups waiting for her.

***

During the drive home, Mary took the puppies from the pasteboard box and held them in her lap. I was surprised they didn't cry or yelp. They actually snuggled together and slept most of the way home. We made a brief stop at a grocery store to pick up some dog food.

Although we had two dog crates the puppies could use, Mary and I couldn't bear the thought of separating the puppies. Not yet. We fed them their first meal of puppy chow and then took them outside. They sniffed around in the grass until finally they … "did their business." We brought them inside and played with them until they got sleepy. Then we put them together in a single crate.

"We'll need larger crates soon because Lab pups grow fast," I said.

Mary nodded as she closed and latched the crate.

We left the room next to the garage—which became known as the Dog Room—passed through the laundry room, and walked through the kitchen and into the living room. Mary settled herself in a recliner and began reading a book by Ken Follett.

I decided to do some research. I turned on my computer and went online to get some advice on raising Lab puppies. After thirty minutes of visiting various sites, I turned to Mary and said, "We may have made a big mistake."

She closed her book and gave me her full attention. "Why do you say that?"

"Well, on one website, the advice was to never get puppies from the same litter. On another website, I read that if you *do* get puppies from the same litter, never get puppies of the same sex because they may fight each other for dominance. Also, there's something called 'littermate syndrome,' which means that the puppies may bond so closely with each other that they'll never completely bond with us."

"I'm not going to worry about all that," laughed Mary. "I'm just going to love them no matter what. You're good at naming dogs. Think about it tonight, and by tomorrow, you should have some good names for them. Goodnight. I'll check on the puppies one more time, and then I'm going to bed."

I went outside and settled into a comfortable chair on the deck. The warm night settled around me. Crickets chirped, and a bullfrog croaked from the nearby New River. Moths of various sizes hovered around the dim lightbulb behind my chair. I smiled as I remembered the dogs I'd owned in the past and their names.

When I was in the third grade, my grandfather had given me a puppy I named "Ranger" after my TV hero, the Lone Ranger. After college, I had owned a purebred collie I named "Serendipity Daisy." While we were dating, Mary had found a tiny black-and-white puppy all alone in the forest near the house she was renting. I named him "Solo" because he was found all by himself.

As Solo aged, I felt he needed a friend and protector. Along came a fast-growing, lively puppy I called "Spirit." Spirit—a cross between an Australian Cattle Dog and a Samoyed—had a fluffy blue merle coat. Spirit took her role of Solo's protector seriously and would let no dog, big or small, harm the eleven-year-old dog.

Next came a beautiful, sensitive yellow Labrador retriever. Her first owner, one of our neighbors, had gotten a job in Winston-Salem. The apartment he rented in the city would not allow pets. He gave the six-month-old Lab to me. Because of her milky color, I named her "Buttermilk."

As I sat alone in the gathering darkness, I reflected on the deaths of my dogs. Dogs have relatively short lives. Ranger, a woods-wandering farm dog, died due to contracting rabies. Ranger exhibited the common symptoms: aggression, throat and jaw paralysis with mouth foaming, a staggering gait, and weakness in the hind legs. Unfortunately, during my boyhood, the rabies vaccine was seldom given to farm dogs, so my grandfather had to shoot Ranger. I was away at school when Ranger's life ended. My grandfather had buried the dog before I got home. Ranger was only five years old. Daisy, my collie, developed a taste for chickens and was shot by a chicken farmer. She came home wounded, bleeding, and dying. She was seven years old. I couldn't blame the farmer; he was just protecting his livelihood. Spirit, the Samoyed-Cattle Dog mix, inherited a strong herding instinct from both her parents and developed a bad habit of chasing cars. Impulsively, she was trying to chase and herd automobiles, and one of the vehicles ran over her. She was killed instantly. Spirit was not quite two years old when she passed. Solo, the foundling pup, lived for more than twelve years and died of old age. Buttermilk, our Lab, had reached the age of eight when she died from a sudden illness.

Before going to bed, I decided to visit the dog room and say goodnight to the puppies. They were sound asleep. The plump puppy was resting her head on her littermate's shoulder. I could barely detect their soft puppy snores. "What shall I name you little ladies?" I whispered. Some names came to mind: Stormy and Sunshine, Autumn and Summer, Maggie and Millie, Honey and Sugar, and Holly and Dolly. I wasn't satisfied with any of them.

I knelt down next to the puppy crate. The pleasant smell of young puppies surrounded me. I wanted to pet them, but I refrained because I didn't want to wake them. Like Buttermilk, the little Labs were creamy white in color. "I wish you two little ones could have known Buttermilk," I whispered. "She was the perfect Labrador retriever. I hope you grow up to be like her. Goodnight, pups. I'm going to bed."

* * *

There are two types of Labrador retrievers: the English Lab and the American Lab. English Labs are stocky dogs, sturdy and solid. Their bodies are broad and heavy. The American Lab is generally taller and lankier with a more athletic build. Both kinds of Labs love to swim and retrieve. Although they came from the same litter, our fat puppy was to grow up to be a fine example of the English

Lab while her robust sister had the characteristics of the American Lab. I'd seen chocolate and black Labrador retrievers, but I preferred the looks of the yellow Lab. Yellow Labs come in a variety of shades: pale yellow, almost white; light cream; medium yellow; dark yellow; and reddish-brown, sometimes called "fox red." Our pups' coats were light cream like Buttermilk's had been.

Mary and I had just recently lost Buttermilk. After coming home from a week-long trip to Myrtle Beach, we discovered our dog would neither eat nor drink water. I called the pet sitter who had taken care of her while we were away and was informed that Buttermilk had eaten well the night before. Nonetheless, the dog's abdomen was swollen and felt hot to the touch. The Labrador breed is stoic, but we could see the pain in her eyes. After several trips to the veterinarian and many blood tests, it was determined that Buttermilk had pancreatic cancer. "Pancreatic cancer is deadly," said our veterinarian, "and it can spread rapidly to other organs. You may take Buttermilk home. I'll send some pain relievers home with you." Two weeks passed, and Buttermilk's pain was increasing. She would not eat and would only drink small amounts of water. Our vet recommended that she be put down although she was only eight years old. I had hoped for many more years with Buttermilk. We had been such a happy family.

My wife and I lived near the New River. Buttermilk had loved to leap into the river and retrieve tennis balls. Her other passion was eating, a typical trait in Labs. Her active life kept her lean and agile. Buttermilk's sensitive nose enabled her to track down a tennis ball thrown into the thick woods just below our house. With her nose inches from the ground, she would run in wide circles at first, and then the circles would get smaller and smaller until she located the tennis ball.

Mary and I enjoyed hiking the trail from Bass Lake up to Flattop Manor, also called Moses Cone Manor. The magnificent twenty-three-room house is located near the town of Blowing Rock and just off the Blue Ridge Parkway. The elevation of the land upon which the mansion was built is around forty-five hundred feet. Below the mansion, the winding trails, which included switchbacks, were designed by Moses H. Cone and were called carriage roads. Moses Cone, who died in 1908, was a wealthy North Carolina textile industrialist, a philanthropist, and a conservationist. Cone Manor is now part of the Moses H. Cone Memorial Park, which is run by the National Park Service.

When we walked the trails leading up to the Cone mansion, Buttermilk enjoyed trotting along with us. If she thought we were walking too slowly, she would run ahead of us, stopping to sniff if she found an interesting scent. Sometimes, we encountered horses and riders on the trail. When she spotted horses, our yellow Lab would gallop back to us and sit beside us as we stood off the trail to let the horses pass by. She never barked or did anything that might have spooked the horses. On horseback, several riders stopped to praise our well-mannered Labrador retriever.

Once, while we were descending the trail from Flattop Manor down to Bass Lake, Buttermilk lifted her nose with both nostrils twitching. She wagged her tail, barked, and bounded down a steep bank. We watched as she continued her downward trek until she disappeared into the thick rhododendrons. Several minutes passed and Mary became worried. "Kent, why don't you call her? She might get lost on one of the switchback trails."

"Don't worry. I think I see her. She's climbing back up to us."

Peering down the hillside, we saw a bit of creamy yellow amid the greenery and flowers. Our Lab was climbing the steep hillside toward us. When she arrived, she dropped a worn tennis ball at my feet. Then, exhausted, she lay beside the trail, panting in the green grass. After a few minutes of rest, her energy returned, and she trotted ahead of us as we descended the trail. In her jaws, she carried her doggy treasure, a prized tennis ball.

**

Buttermilk had ruled our household with the gentle power of love. If you've ever owned a Lab, you know why Labrador retrievers are the most popular breed in the United States. After our Buttermilk's death, Mary and I decided to get another Lab. That was how we ended up with our two Lab puppies.

"Have you decided on names for the pups?" asked Mary as we sipped our morning coffee on our deck. Our deck chairs were cushioned and very comfortable. The little Labs nibbled at Mary's bedroom slippers as we talked. The morning sunshine turned the pups' blonde coats to a soft, golden color.

"Yes, if you agree, we'll call them 'Bonnie' and 'Belle.' Belle is the fat puppy."

"Those names are perfect," Mary declared as she reached down and scratched Bonnie behind her ears. Then she picked up Belle and placed the puppy in her lap. I did the same with Bonnie. Only minutes before, we had laughed at the pups' determined but unsuccessful effort to climb the single step from the deck into the living room. Within days, however, Bonnie and Belle had solved the step problem and were able to negotiate all the steps on our property.

When we fed them puppy chow, we noticed how they wagged their small, otter-like tails as they ate. When full-grown, those tails would become rudders as Bonnie and Belle swam in the New River. The puppies shared a large water bowl left over from our days with Buttermilk. Sometimes, both pups would climb into the water bowl, splash around until they were soaked, and then sit down in the bowl. Bonnie panted as Belle licked and nibbled her sister's waterlogged ear.

"What's cuter than a Lab puppy?" Mary asked, smiling down at Bonnie and Belle.

"I don't know," I said.

"*Two* Lab puppies!" laughed Mary. She took a photograph of Bonnie and Belle lounging in their water-bowl-turned-swimming pool.

As Bonnie and Belle grew older, they began chewing on things. We bought chew toys that were labeled "indestructible," but the pups made short work of them. An indestructible rubber chew toy would be chewed up and often swallowed within minutes. At four months, the young Labs began to terrorize the neighborhood. Looking for things to chew, they invaded nearby porches, decks, and garages. We would often get irate phone calls from our neighbors.

"Come get your dogs! They are chewing up our deck furniture!" barked a neighbor, whose property bordered the New River.

"I'll pay for any damages," I said. Leashes in hand, I ran down the driveway to retrieve my immature retrievers.

The next day, I got a call from another neighbor. "Your dogs are in our garage! They've chewed up our garden hose. You'll have to pay for a replacement. Come quickly, now they are gnawing on our lawnmower tires!"

We asked our neighbors to keep their garage doors closed until Bonnie and Belle got older. We bought expandable gates for our neighbors' decks and porches. We replaced two garden hoses, one catcher's mitt, a pair of tennis shoes, and three deck chairs. The most expensive replacement was a hammock Bonnie and Belle had chewed until it was beyond repair. Their hammock-munching had cost Mary and me over one hundred and fifty dollars.

If the pups heard children playing in the neighborhood, they bounded off to investigate. Our Labs *loved* children. When Belle was eleven months old, she came home with a rope around her neck. Mary and I discovered that a little neighbor girl, just beyond toddlerhood, loved to ride Belle as if she were a pony. The sturdy Belle, nearing her full growth, was a willing playmate.

On the occasion of our Labs' first Thanksgiving, I was in the kitchen surrounded by agreeable cooking aromas. When I looked out the kitchen window, I noticed a curious sight. Bonnie was running up the driveway, pursued by a neighbor dressed in a suit. In her jaws, Bonnie clutched what turned out to be an unopened champagne bottle. The gentleman and I managed to catch Bonnie and take the full bottle of champagne from her.

"Why in the world would a dog carry off a bottle of champagne?" asked our neighbor, Rick Spears, who was the owner of Spears Diamonds, a jewelry store in Blowing Rock.

"I'm afraid Bonnie is an alcoholic, Rick. She goes to her first Alcoholics Anonymous meeting next week."

He chuckled and petted Bonnie's head. Bonnie licked his hand. When she panted, it looked as if the dog were laughing with Rick. There were no hard feelings.

Our closest neighbor, David Hawkins, had two dogs. One was a six-year-old golden retriever named Duke, and the other was a black-and-white border collie puppy named Riley. Duke was reserved when it came to playing with Bonnie and Belle. Conversely, Riley was an enthusiastic playmate. The three dogs barked at each other, pawed at each other, and pulled at dog toys in a three-way tug-of-war. They chased tails, played keep-away with tennis balls, and bowled each other over with chest bumps. Sometimes they rolled together in the grass, morphing into one big, blonde, black-and-white ball of fur. One pup would finally woof, signaling it was time to rest. The threesome would lie down close together in the lawn, panting with their pink tongues hanging from their white-toothed jaws. If Duke was nearby, he would join them and lie down in the shade near them, but he regarded the pups as middle-aged parents might regard their wayward teenage children. He refused all invitations to play with the pups.

On Duke's collar were his tags, but the dog's hair around his neck was so thick, the collar and tags had disappeared from sight. In the summertime, the golden retriever loved to follow canoes as the riders paddled their water crafts down the nearby New River. Sometimes, the dog ended up far away, and a telephone call from a family down the river would pinpoint Duke's location. David grumbled, but he always took his truck and picked up the wandering canine. On a few occasions, I went with him to pick up his big retriever. As soon as Duke saw David's pickup truck, he ran toward it, barking and wagging his tail, overjoyed to be rescued. Once, Duke disappeared for three weeks. There was no phone call reporting Duke's whereabouts.

David called me to ask if I'd seen Duke. "No, I haven't seen him for days," I said, "but I'd be glad to ride along with you to search for him. Two pairs of eyes are better than one."

David, with me riding shotgun, drove along the paved highways and gravel roads that paralleled the New River, but there was no sign of Duke. He stopped at several houses, asking if anyone had seen a big golden retriever.

No luck.

David dropped me off back at my house. As I got out of his truck, I said, "Call me if you hear anything about Duke."

"I'll do that. Thanks for your help, Kent. I'm surprised how much I miss the old dog. It's goin' on four weeks since he first disappeared. I'm afraid we may never see him again. My kids cry at the mention of his name."

After Duke had been missing for five weeks, there came a long-distance phone call from Atlanta, Georgia, reporting that Duke had been found. Yes, Duke had somehow made his way from the Tar Heel State to the Peach State. I wondered if David would drive all the way to Atlanta to rescue his wandering dog.

"I never would've driven to Atlanta to pick up Duke if the girls hadn't overheard my telephone conversation," said David. He had three small daughters who loved their dogs, both Duke and Riley. The little girls also showered Bonnie and Belle with affection when they visited to play with Riley.

Standing outside on my house's wraparound deck, I had overheard David's out-of-doors conversation with his daughters. Of course, the topic of the discussion was the missing golden retriever.

"Oh, Daddy, you must bring Duke home," said the eldest of his three daughters. "I'll ride to 'Lanta with you to keep you company."

"Duke is the best doggie ever!" declared his youngest daughter. "He might be scared and hungwy." Then she began to cry, which caused his middle daughter to cry too. Soon, all three girls were crying.

David knelt down and hugged his three daughters all at once, in one embrace. "All right! All right. I'll go get him tomorrow," said the outnumbered father.

David gave me the details of Duke's adventure shortly after he arrived home with the golden retriever sitting in the dark-blue pickup truck's passenger seat. When the passenger door was opened, Duke leaped to the ground and was quickly surrounded by three golden-haired little girls, hugging and petting him. The smallest girl climbed on Duke's back and repeated that Duke was "the best doggie ever." Duke's canine buddy, Riley, who was barking, whining, and licking, also gave Duke a warm welcome.

David, after doing some amateur detective work, reported to me that Duke had gotten lost because he followed a flotilla of four canoes and one kayak down the New River. Swimming beside the largest canoe, Duke was hoping for treats. The paddlers threw a few treats to the dog, which he gobbled up. When the group of nine vacationers stopped for their picnic lunches, the golden retriever was, no doubt, given more food. The big dog followed the travelers to their destination, where they began loading up the canoes and kayak. Duke jumped up into the bed of a pickup truck, where he rested beside a large canoe. Unable to find the collar under the wet, matted ruff around Duke's neck, thus assuming he was a stray, the canoe owners, a couple from Charlotte, decided to adopt Duke and take him home with them.

According to David, the golden retriever seemed happy enough in his new Charlotte home, but the couple's other two pets, a Ragdoll cat and a Boston terrier puppy, were terrified by the presence of the large intruder. With the arrival of Duke, the Ragdoll and the black-and-white terrier spent most of their time cowering under the bed in the master bedroom. When Jimmy Buffett came to Charlotte for an outdoor concert, the Charlotte couple hatched a plan and put it into action. On the night of the concert, they called Duke, and he jumped into the bed of their pickup. The couple, using strong tape, fastened two handwritten signs to the sides of their pickup. Both signs read, "Free purebred golden retriever dog! We can no longer keep him. Answers to the name of 'Lucky.' Free dog!"

Although Lucky—better known as Duke—howled during Jimmy Buffett's performance of "Margaritaville," a passerby, who lived in the Atlanta suburbs and owned an aging golden retriever, decided to take Duke home with him. He took the dog from the pickup truck bed and transferred him to the backseat of his car. He then began the long drive from Charlotte to Atlanta. The day after he arrived, he decided to bathe his new golden retriever in his family's bathtub. During the drying process, he noticed Duke's ruff-hidden collar and dog tags. He immediately called David, and soon Duke was returned to his Watauga County home and the three little girls who adored the dog. David's wife, Helen, took several photographs of her daughters welcoming home their wandering retriever.

Bonnie and Belle never noticed Duke's absence. They were too busy playing with Riley. Too soon, it seemed, the three dogs were more than one year old. Like Duke, Bonnie and Belle began to wander. They didn't follow canoes, but they followed children in the neighborhood. Once, we discovered that they had crossed the river bridge and the highway beyond the river. After a long and increasingly frantic search, Mary and I found the Labs frolicking in a lawn three miles away from home. A little girl seated in a lawn chair was blowing bubbles as Bonnie and Belle jumped and snapped at the floating bubbles, bursting them in midair. We called our Labs and they came instantly, jumping through our car's open rear door and into the backseat. We waved to the bubble-blowing child and took our dogs home.

There was another time when Mary and I left Bonnie and Belle alone because we were going to meet friends at a local Boone restaurant, The Red Onion. Bonnie was lying under a shade tree, chewing on a tennis ball. Belle was nowhere in sight.

"She's probably behind the house, digging in my flower garden," laughed Mary. Belle, although she was now two years old and beyond the mischief of puppyhood, had recently dug up a newly planted rhododendron bush. Bonnie had been her accomplice in the crime.

After spending two hours at the restaurant, we drove home in the darkening twilight. Coming up the driveway, we saw Bonnie, who looked like a white ghost in our headlights' glow, jumping around and wagging her tail furiously. Bonnie was always ecstatic when we came home. I drove the car into the garage, carefully avoiding the overjoyed pooch. Mary and I exited the vehicle and played with Bonnie for a moment. We then called for Belle.

No response.

We called for Belle again and again. She did not come to us. This was unusual because Belle usually joined Bonnie in her homecoming dance of delight. We circled the house, calling in all directions for our missing dog.

"I'm worried," said Mary. "Belle never leaves home without Bonnie by her side."

The search began.

First, we searched the house. Then, in our Subaru, we drove to every nearby neighbor's house and asked, "Have you seen Belle?" No one had seen her. We drove across the river bridge and stopped at a house where we had once located Bonnie and Belle when they were five months old. They had followed neighborhood children there. We rang the doorbell. An elderly man answered in his pajamas.

When we asked him if he'd seen Belle, our Labrador retriever, he said, "No, I ain't seen neither one of them dogs since they was pups. I remember that they chewed up the legs on one of my deck chairs. You better keep them dang Labs on your own property, or they'll get shot!"

He slammed the door before I had a chance to remind him that I had paid him for the damages. Mary shivered when she heard those words: "they'll get shot." Sundown had turned to dusk and then to darkness. We drove back to our house.

"What if Belle's been shot or run over?" asked Mary. "She's a beautiful dog. What if she's been stolen?"

"We'll search more tomorrow," I said. "Besides, we've been gone over an hour. She may be waiting for us at home."

As I pulled the Subaru into our driveway, I noticed something red in the grass beside the pavement. It was Belle's collar. I didn't tell Mary because it would've only added to her fears. Besides, although older now, Bonnie and Belle still roughhoused with Riley, the border collie. During their boisterous play, Riley enjoyed tugging at the Labs' collars and often succeeded in pulling them off. Wandering collarless across the river on the highway, Belle might have been picked up. I recalled Duke's adventure and then pushed the memory out of my mind.

I parked the Subaru in the garage, and then Mary and I exited the vehicle. We watched Bonnie tuck her tail and circle the car in her quivering dance of delight. She barked a joyous welcome. Bonnie's bark was deep-throated while the missing Belle's bark was shrill and high-pitched.

Then, remembering the exploits of the TV dogs, Lassie and Rin Tin Tin, I said, "Bonnie, where is Belle? Help us find her. Bonnie, find Belle. Go on, girl, find Belle!"

Bonnie perked her ears and turned her head to one side. She ran to the front door and scratched. That was her signal that she wanted to go inside. We opened the door, and Bonnie ran inside, lay down by the fireplace, and began chewing on a doggie toy. She seemed unconcerned about Belle's disappearance.

Then we heard a sharp bark and a whimpering sound. "That's Belle!" I yelled happily. "She's somewhere in the house!"

"Yes, but where? We've already looked everywhere," said Mary.

In our house, every bedroom had a bathroom. In the smallest bedroom, there was a tiny bathroom with no bathtub, just a shower. In the undersized bathroom, we found Belle. Somehow, she had managed to push the bathroom door open and then closed it behind her. Belle had imprisoned herself. Of course, she was overjoyed to see us. Mary knelt and hugged Belle, and she was rewarded with dozens of Lab smooches. We brought Belle into the living room, where she greeted Bonnie.

"Belle has been cooped up for hours. We'd better send her outside so she can do her business," said Mary.

"Yes, Belle is overdue for a visit to her outdoor toilet."

We opened the front door, and both dogs raced outside and began barking at God knows what. Their noses were working overtime, sniffing the cool, mountain air. After a few minutes, Bonnie and Belle settled down, and the barking ceased. Our Labs stayed outside for about an hour and then began pawing and whining at the front door. We brought them inside and gave them bone-shaped doggy treats. Then we took them down to a room that was originally designed to be Mary's craft room but was now the dog room. Bonnie and Belle went into their separate crates and began licking their paws, a ritual that was a prelude to sleep. Mary and I went up the two steps that led to the laundry room and then negotiated the single step that took us into the kitchen.

"Kent, I'm exhausted. Let's go to bed."

"Yes, Belle has given us a long and tumultuous day. I'm sleepy too."

***

As the years passed, Bonnie and Belle swam, splashed, and frolicked in the New River below our house. They fetched hundreds of tennis balls. They were at our sides as Mary and I hiked the many North Carolina mountain trails near the towns of West Jefferson, Boone, and Blowing Rock. Although Bonnie and Belle loved river water, they didn't like to be out in the rain and would demand to be let inside during the mildest of rainstorms. Thunder terrified them, as did the distant sound of gunshots. Unfortunately, across the river on a ridge, lived a retired Highway Patrol officer who enjoyed regular target practice. The sound of both thunder and gunshots brought the dogs inside where they stretched out and panted inches away from my feet.

During most winters, Watauga County got more than its share of snow, and the two dogs were thrilled with every snowfall—the deeper the better. They nosed the snow, sticking their black noses deep into the white softness. Belle often chose a steep bank and, on her tummy, she slid down the bank as if she were sledding. Seemingly tireless, she galloped up the bank and glided down again and again. Sometimes, Bonnie would join her, but Bonnie's favorite snow-day activity was to roll around in the snow. With all four legs in the air, she would wriggle in the snow as if scratching an itch on her back. Chasing each other, the dogs plowed through snow drifts, and after their play, they would come inside so wet that one would think they'd been submerged in deep river water. They enjoyed being toweled dry.

During one particularly cold winter, with the daytime temperatures rising to no more than eight degrees and then plummeting to near zero at night, the New River became clogged with floating chunks of ice. After a week, the biting wind, coupled with the numbing cold, froze the river so solidly that the waterway could support foot traffic. From our deck, Mary and I, wrapped in long, wool coats with toboggans on our heads, watched three teenagers skate on the thickly frozen New River. Our gloved hands held coffee cups of steaming hot chocolate, and we sipped the warming drink as we watched the scene below us. The three youths on the river had no ice skates; they skated with slick-bottomed boots and shoes. I had done so myself, several times, as a youngster, growing up on a farm near the New River in Ashe County. A black-and-white dog was with the young people. It was Riley, our neighbor's border collie.

When Bonnie and Belle saw Riley and the three kids, we couldn't contain them. They ran off the deck and down to the ice-covered river. Barks and laughter signaled that both dogs and youngsters were having a good time.

"Should we put on our heavy boots and join them?" I asked. "The ice is thick enough to support us."

"No, we're a bit too old for that kind of play," smiled Mary. She took my gloved hand in hers and reminded me of last winter. On the day after Christmas, I had slipped on a layer of ice that covered our driveway. I had hurt my back and missed two days of work. "We're not kids anymore, Kent." She kissed me on the cheek with hot-chocolate-warmed lips.

She was right, of course. We went inside and had a breakfast of coffee, waffles with maple syrup, scrambled eggs, and orange juice. After an hour had passed, I heard whining and scratching at the front door. I opened the door. Bonnie and Belle came inside the warm house and lay down on their mats in front of the flickering gas fireplace. Within minutes, both dogs were snoring peacefully. The doggie snores were relaxing, and I, in my recliner, and Mary, on our couch under a woolen blanket, joined the dogs in a deep January slumber.

***

The winter months passed slowly in North Carolina's mountains, but soon it was February, and, outside, rhododendron leaves tightened like arthritic green fingers that were partially gloved by snowflakes left behind by last week's snowstorm. Several windless days had passed, and soft snow had spiraled downward in great, fluffy flakes. The snowflakes settled on the leafless trees, covering the bare limbs and trunks with delicate, cottony garments. Neighboring houses and farms snuggled comfortably under a silver and white bedspread. A windstorm arrived on Valentine's Day. Strong snow-blowing gusts caused simple objects—mailboxes, wheelbarrows, fence posts, and deck furniture—to take on unusual shapes that were sometimes comical and sometimes eerie.

Temperatures plummeted. One night, before I went to bed, I checked the indoor/outdoor thermometer. The temperature outside registered eight degrees; the next morning, the temperature had risen to ten degrees. A full week of cold weather passed. The New River was solidly frozen. The cold weather didn't bother Bonnie and Belle, though. They played outside, crunching through the ice-covered snow as if it were a summer day.

In early March, the frozen river was beginning to thaw. Although the temperatures still hovered in the low to mid-twenties at night, the March days were sunny during the first week of the month. Our neighbor, Betty Faircloth, decided to take a walk with her black-and-brown collie-sized dog, Moxie. Bonnie and Belle, who were visiting Moxie at the time, decided to tag along. Riley, the border collie, came running to join the dogs and Betty.

Mary and I were visiting friends in Ashe County, and it wasn't unusual for Bonnie and Belle to visit Betty and Moxie when we were away from the house. Betty loved dogs, and she was glad to have Bonnie, Belle, and Riley along for the walk. Betty told me that Moxie led the way, and the other dogs trailed behind her. Now and then, the dogs would stop and sniff the bushes, sometimes marking the snow-covered ground with their urine. According to Betty, everything was normal for the first ten minutes of the walk. Then things went awry.

Riley lifted his nose and smelled the air. Something across the frozen river had caught his attention. He scampered across the still solid stream. Belle followed as the forty-five-pound border collie trotted across the ice, but the seventy-five-pound Belle, when she was halfway across the river, plunged through the ice. Belle clung to the ice with her front paws as a semicircle of freezing water rushed around her. She barked and then began whining.

Betty panicked. She told me she had felt a sharp pain in her chest. After a few deep breaths, the pain subsided. "I ran back to my house and called you," said Betty. "I knew that Belle couldn't keep holding on in that cold water. I got no answer at your house, so I called David Hawkins. I told him where Belle was and then got in my car and drove down the river road until I could see Belle still hanging on to the solid ice. She had slipped further into the river. She had stopped whining and was silent. The other three dogs, Bonnie, Moxie, and Riley, were barking and howling on the riverbank."

David, who worked in the construction industry, had spent the day supervising and helping some of his men as they assembled a deck around a home in Boone, near Appalachian State University. Drink in hand, he was resting in a recliner next to his blazing fireplace when his telephone rang. "I'll be right there!" he told Betty. He slipped on his work boots and ran, without his winter coat, to his truck.

According to Betty, David arrived and quickly surveyed the situation. Using his heavy boots, he stomped through the ice until he was more than knee-deep in river water. Raising his legs, he kicked at the ice as he created a path toward Belle. In waist-high water, he battered the ice with his strong forearms. "Hold on, Belle!" he shouted. With the freezing water just under his armpits, he tried to grab Belle by the collar. She was collarless, so he grabbed her around the chest and pulled her toward him. Holding the trembling dog tight, he made his way back toward the shore through the watery path he had created.

Both man and dog were shivering when they reached the safety of the shore. David placed the shuddering Belle on her side in the snow. The dog didn't try to stand, but her tail wagged stiffly.

"Help me get Belle into my car," said Betty. "Kent and Mary aren't at home. I'll take her to my place and dry her off with towels. Then I'll take her in and warm her up by the fireplace. Bonnie, Moxie, and Riley are already headed for home. You need to get home, too, David. You must be freezing."

"I ... I'm ... I'm a-all right. B-B-Belle is one l-l-lucky dog," he said. "But I g-g-gotta get home quick. The wind's p-p-pickin' up!"

Belle was lifted into Betty's car where she began whining. Then David, shaking in his wet clothes, ran with waterlogged boots to his pickup and drove to his house, which was, fortunately, nearby. Within ten minutes, Belle was warming herself by Betty's fireplace. In addition to the heat of the hearth, Belle was dried with Betty's electric hairdryer. Betty gave Belle and Moxie two dog biscuits for treats.

Later that night, when Mary and I got home, Belle and Bonnie welcomed us at the garage door. Belle barked and wagged her tail furiously, and Bonnie scampered in circles around our parked car. Everything seemed normal. The next morning, when Betty called, we learned of Belle's brush with death.

I thanked Betty many times during our telephone conversation, but she said, "David is the one you should thank. He risked his life to save Belle."

"I'll call him right away. I hope he's at home," I said. When his telephone rang, David answered. I thanked him for saving my dog's life.

"Think nothin' of it, Kent. I will say that there are a few fellers that I woulda left hangin' on the ice in the middle of the river. But I couldn't let Belle drown. It didn't take no courage on my part. When I saw the fix Belle was in, I didn't think about it. I just jumped in the river and worked my way out to where she was holdin' on."

After the rescue, Belle would watch for David to come home from work. When his big Chevrolet pickup pulled into his driveway, usually around six o'clock in the evening, she would race to greet him. He would kneel down and hug her. She would bark, lick his face, and whine with happiness.

"Do you think Belle knows you saved her life?" I asked David one day.

"Oh, she knows, all right. Dogs are a whole lot smarter than we give 'em credit for," he said. He then spent some time petting *his* dogs, Duke and Riley.

* * *

When Bonnie and Belle reached the age of ten, I noticed they were slowing down. Sprains took longer to heal, and fatty lumps—called "lipomas" by our vet—formed under their skin. On long walks, they seemed more cautious about exploring new trails. Our Labs slept more during the day, and Mary and I were reluctant to wake them, sensing they probably needed their rest. We decided to do some research on the longevity of Labrador retrievers. Mary discovered that Labs typically live ten to twelve years. My investigations were more hopeful, suggesting the normal lifespan was twelve to almost thirteen years.

"Let's do our best to keep them happy and healthy during their final years, but let's not allow them to suffer as they age," said Mary. She knelt and hugged both dogs, Bonnie on her left, Belle on her right. She was rewarded with canine kisses.

***

When the dogs reached the age of eleven, I considered their lives with Mary and me. During my contemplation, the Labs were sleeping on separate mats in front of the fireplace. They were dreaming. Belle's legs were twitching, suggesting she was chasing something—a squirrel or rabbit—through dreamland. Her lips drew back, exposing her aging, yellow teeth. Bonnie was in the midst of a happy dream. Her eyes were closed, but her tail was wagging, thumping her mat with considerable force. She stretched her still-muscular hind legs. Simultaneously, Bonnie and Belle sighed and drifted further into a quiet, deep slumber.

Their lifetimes had been spent splashing in the warm waters of the New River on sunny summer days. In the fall, the cooler weather invigorated them as they chased each other—and their playmate Riley—through colorful piles of raked leaves. On snowy winter mornings, Bonnie and Belle couldn't wait to get out of their crates and explore a strange new world created by the snowfall. Springtime rains forced them to take shelter under the covered portion of our house's deck. When the rain slackened, the two dogs left the deck to smell the new flowers pushing up through the moist soil. If they found some shoots of grass to their liking, the dogs nibbled on them. When they encountered a rain puddle, they dug into it madly as if they were searching for an underground source of water. Like most Labrador retrievers, they had healthy appetites. We fed them a larger meal in the mornings and a lesser meal at suppertime.

"They've had good lives," said Mary one morning after the dogs had been fed in the dog room. "They've never gone hungry, and they've always had a warm place to sleep."

I nodded and put my arm around my wife's shoulder as we watched Bonnie and Belle limp through the dog room's open door. Bonnie favored her right foreleg, and Belle's hind legs had been stiff and sore for days. I pulled Mary closer to me and wiped a tear from her cheek. We knew our time left with Bonnie and Belle was limited.

***

I held up two small blue plastic bottles with white plastic caps. One read, "FOR: Belle/Canine. Give two capsules by mouth once at night as needed for pain. Gabapentin, 300 mg per capsule." The other plastic bottle read, "FOR: Belle/Canine. Give one tablet by mouth once daily with food as needed for pain. Carprofen Caplets 75 mg." The pain medications helped Belle get a good night's sleep, at least for a while.

Belle had developed a large, fatty tumor just in front of her left hind leg. The tumor was starting to impede her walking and her ability to get up after sleeping. Another lump was forming on her right shoulder, seemingly under a muscle. Going down or up two steps was difficult for her. When she stumbled, she yelped in pain. Her eyes were clouded, and she seemed confused as she gazed around a familiar room. She demanded more petting, pawing at our legs for attention. Sometimes, she couldn't get up from her mat, and Mary and I struggled to get her on her feet. She had also gained weight. She weighed more than eighty pounds, but we often called her "Little Belle" because she was somewhat smaller than Bonnie. I sometimes gave Bonnie some pain medicine because she was arthritic like Belle. However, Bonnie's condition was much better than Belle's.

"Kent, our Little Belle is suffering. She's on her last legs. We have to make a decision about her. I've made my decision. I'm just waiting on you to decide."

"I know. I just can't seem to let her go, Mary. Her appetite is good ...," I choked back the tears. "She ... Once we get her on her feet, she can ...."

Mary looked at me with gloomy eyes. "I'm going to the dog room to clean the crates. Belle had an accident in her crate last night. I'll put a fresh mat down for her."

I took a deep breath and said, "I'll call the veterinarian and describe Belle's condition."

***

After ending my conversation with our veterinarian, I said to Mary, "Doctor Keller says Belle's time has come.

Our dog should be euthanized. She promises to do it very humanely."

"Did you make an appointment?"

"I did."

***

On Belle's last day, we fed her chunks of cut-up beef, took turns petting her, and whispered that we loved her in her left ear. By now, she was deaf in her right ear. The tired, old dog responded with as much love as she could muster. Belle licked our hands and cheeks with her warm tongue.

When the time came, Mary and I helped Belle to her feet and led her into the garage. It took both of us to lift her into the Subaru's backseat. Bonnie wanted to come along, but we left her behind. Mary drove and I sat in the backseat with Belle. Mary drove slowly. As always, Belle sat up and stuck her nose out the open window to pick up the scents we humans couldn't smell. I patted her back, and she wagged her tail feebly.

Mary pulled the Subaru into the Blue Ridge Pet Care parking lot. At this point, Bonnie and Belle always had begun whining, but Belle didn't whine this time. Dr. Karen Keller, a plump woman who had been our veterinarian for many years, came outside to the car with her assistant, a young man in his early twenties. The young man pushed a gurney up to the side of our car.

"Hello, Belle. You are such a good dog," said Dr. Keller. Belle pushed her nose further out the window so Dr. Keller could pet her.

"Kent, I'm going to give Belle a shot that will make her very sleepy. Soon, she'll be in a deep sleep. If you want, you may pet her until she loses consciousness. Then Jeff and I will put her on the gurney and take her inside. During her deep sleep, we will give her a shot that will stop her heart. You've already made the arrangements to have Belle cremated."

Then I wavered. I almost said, "Let's give Belle a few more days or perhaps a week and see how she does."

However, I said nothing ....

The shot was given.

Saying they would be back in about ten minutes, Dr. Keller and Jeff went inside. I sat beside Belle and petted her. Mary left the driver's seat and stood outside, stroking Belle through the open rear window. I felt our dog's muscles relax. Mary was crying, and I was trying not to weep. Belle sighed and moved slightly, as if repositioning her body for comfort. As I stroked Belle's shoulders, I noticed the old dog's coat had retained the smooth softness of youth.

Too soon, Dr. Keller and Jeff returned, opened the Subaru's rear door, and placed Belle on the gurney. Pushing the gurney, Jeff followed Dr. Keller through a door marked, "Employees Only."

I thought I saw Belle wag her tail one last time.

I couldn't be sure.

***

I drove the Subaru home. Mary and I did not speak. She dabbed at her eyes with a tissue. Bonnie was waiting for us beside the garage door. She performed her dance of delight and sniffed around the car. I assumed she was looking for her sister, Belle.

We fed Bonnie, and she ate with her usual gusto. She didn't seem saddened by Belle's departure, but, to this day, she has never slept on Belle's mat nor entered Belle's crate. I have seen Bonnie sit at the top of the driveway, ears perked and nose twitching, as if she's waiting for Belle's return. Mary says she's simply waiting for Riley, who is now an old dog, too, but still comes to visit occasionally.

Mary and I took Bonnie to the veterinarian recently. She was deemed healthy except for nuclear sclerosis, a bluish haze that develops in the lens of an older dog's eyes, mild tartar on her worn teeth, and multiple lipoma-like growths along with numerous warts. She is arthritic and has muscle atrophy in her hips.

Like Belle, Bonnie has been prescribed pain relievers, gabapentin and carprofen—the same dosages as Belle. Also as Belle did, Bonnie walks with a severe limp and has trouble getting up from her mat. Belle lived to be twelve years and six days old. Bonnie is currently twelve years and five months old.

***

Last night, I had a dream about Bonnie and Belle. In my dream, they were adolescent puppies, and Mary and I—with tennis balls in our pockets—had taken them down to the New River. In the dream, Mary and I were twelve years younger. I could easily throw the balls far up the river or all the way across the river. We were teaching the Lab pups to fetch. Again and again we threw the balls, and again and again our Labs fetched them and dropped them at our feet. They settled back on their haunches and panted, showing pink tongues and sharp white puppy teeth. Then Mary threw the ball upstream for Bonnie, and I threw the ball downstream for Belle. Bonnie returned, but Belle continued to swim downstream until she disappeared around a bend in the river. Mary and I called for Belle, but she was gone.

That was when I woke up.

The air-conditioned bedroom was cool, but I was sweating. I slipped silently from the bed to avoid waking Mary. I went outside and sat on a deck chair. The stars were out, and a full moon was reflected in the New River's calm waters. In one corner of the deck, I saw Belle's favorite mat where she often basked in the morning sunlight. I pictured her resting there, yawning and stretching. I'd never owned a dog with a gentler spirit than Belle. I wondered again—as I had many times in the past months—if I should have given her a few more days or a few more weeks of life.

I went back inside and made my way down to the dog room. I noticed I had neglected to close the door leading to the garage, so I closed it. Next to Belle's empty crate, Bonnie was sleeping in her own crate. I knelt down and petted her. She awakened and eyed me curiously. Almost immediately, she lowered her head and went back to sleep. I continued to massage her head and ears.

I looked at Belle's vacant crate and remembered how difficult it had been for her to rise and leave her crate. I remembered her whining and looking at me with sad eyes. I remembered how Mary and I had to help Belle get up from her mat in front of the fireplace. I remembered her stumbling and yelping as she descended steps. For the moment, I decided I had made the right decision for Belle. Bonnie sighed contentedly in her sleep, but, soon, I knew I would have to make a life-and-death decision about her as well.

I made my way through the house and back to the bedroom.

I went to bed and fell sleep.

***

When morning came, I was awakened by the smell of coffee. Outside, I heard Bonnie barking. I waited for Belle's distinctive high-pitched bark. Of course, I didn't hear it. I knew a cup of coffee would help remove the cobwebs from my brain.

I had been told by both my grandfather and father that life was a series of decisions and choices. "Once a decision is made," they had said, "one should move on."

However, I still wondered if I should have given Belle a few more precious days or another week of life. Was the decision I had made for Belle right or wrong?

I guess I'll never know for sure, but I take some comfort in a statement I read just yesterday in a book of quotations:

Often the hardest decisions and the right decisions are the same.

THE PORTRAIT

May I welcome you, sir, to the house of Sattran. Come in, come in and get out of the howling wind. Watch your step, for the stone stairway is icy.

Yes, the original mansion has stood for centuries, but of course, there have been structural additions over the years. The stables were added over sixty years ago. Yes, I agree, from a distance, the house looks like a gray fortress atop this hill.

Sir, I have served the Sattran family for more years than I care to count. Please follow me into the great hall.

May I take your cloak and gloves? No? Well, I do understand. This hall and the surrounding rooms have a chill to them. There is an iciness in this house, but I have grown used to the chill. It sometimes seems that we have but two seasons in these mountains: winter with its freezing gales and deep snow; then a short summer with its dreadful, blood-sucking black flies and a few days of stifling heat; and then the bitter winter begins again. Oh, I admit we have a few days of precious spring warmth, when the flowers sprinkle color at the foot of the mountains. And it is true that the mountains are ablaze with bright hues for about a week or two in the fall. But, often, the spring flowers push up through the snow to reach the sunshine, and the red and yellow leaves of fall are soon scattered by the winter wind.

Has it begun to snow again, sir? Oh, excuse me, sir! It's these old eyes. The traces of silver in your dark hair looked for a moment like snowflakes. My goodness, I wish I were your age again, sir. Looking at me now, you may not believe this, but once I had curly, dark hair, broad shoulders, and good posture. Now my shoulders are boney and thin, and I stoop so much that I can better regard the carpet than the ceiling. My hair, sparse and fine, is pure white as you can see. Each day, I look in the mirror and find a strange old man looking back at me. But we all grow old, don't we, sir?

Ah, your eyes have been captured by the young woman in the portrait, sir. Yes, it is a portrait of the late mistress, Justina Sattran. The painting was commissioned by her father, Petru Sattran, and painted for him by Henric Lecca, who is world-renowned for his distinguished works. The artist acknowledges the portrait that you view is his finest work. His most famous paintings are, of course, "Lovers Strolling Hand-In-Hand" and "The Death Mask." But I have heard him say in this hall, standing right where you stand now, that this portrait of our poor mistress is his greatest work.

Here, let me open the curtains so you may regard the portrait at a better advantage. There now, the setting sun provides perfect light. It so happens that this time of day—that is to say, late afternoon—was Henric Lecca's favorite time to paint. The mistress posed over there in that chair. Yes, the leather chair with the crucifix hanging on the wall above it. Day after day, she sat motionless as the artist worked. I suppose it is difficult for anyone to remain motionless for any length of time. It was especially difficult for the mistress to remain absolutely still. Miss Justina had periods of extreme nervousness, sir. In her early twenties, she began suffering from insomnia. She walked the halls of this mansion at all hours of the night. When she did sleep, nightmares haunted her dreams. I have heard her nighttime screams. She never discussed her night terrors, at least not with me. However, she had amazing powers of concentration for a young woman. She bridled her restless spirit, and this allowed Lecca to finish the portrait.

When she turned twenty-five, I noticed an extreme change in Justina's behavior. She seemed to vacillate between frenetic excitement and general boredom. In the same afternoon, she could move from exhilaration to lassitude. But she was always pleasant and kind to me, no matter what her mood .... That is, until the end. Eventually, as you may have heard in the village, madness overturned her sensibilities.

***

Yes, the portrait is for sale, sir, as are all the paintings in the great hall. Since the death of the mistress, the art treasures collected here by the mistress, her father, and his father have been auctioned for gold and silver. Soon, the entire estate will be up for sale, or, at least, that is the rumor. Having no husband and, therefore, childless, the mistress, in her will, left almost everything to her only living relative: her young cousin, Alexandru Sattran, a man of only twenty-one, and a gentleman who loves the vibrancy of city life. He will not stay here in this wild region of the Carpathian Mountains. He will never manage an estate where the snows linger until late May and where one can hear wolves howl at night.

That reminds me, sir. You had no trouble with wolves as your coach came through the mountains, did you? I ask because, several days ago, a pack of wolves—one report from the village said there were ten or more of them—attacked a coach and its horses about a mile from the village. I was told that among the wolves was one with silver splashes on his dark coat. More vicious and much larger than the others, he was evidently the pack leader for the other wolves showed him deference. The beasts, gaunt and horrible, had no interest in the coach's human cargo. They were intent on crippling the smaller of the two horses pulling the coach. The gray devils tore at the young mare's legs and haunches until she was helpless. The small horse did not fall, but she could not move forward. The coach came to a standstill. The bigger horse, a gelding, untouched by the wolves, reared and struck at the mare's tormentors with deadly hooves. The gelding left two wolves dead in the red snow.

The driver, fearing for the lives of the travelers, managed to cut the dying mare free from the coach. He left the mare to the wolves, while the larger horse strained mightily and pulled the coach into the village. One passenger, looking back at the scene as the coach edged forward, said that the brown mare still stood trembling in the snow even as the wolves began to feed. She fell into the snow when her forelegs were broken and pulled from her body. Then, the ravenous creatures were upon her. The coach rounded a bend in the forest road, and the passenger saw no more of the carnage.

Indeed, sir, it *was* a close call, but the passengers, the driver, and the gelding all survived. The only loss was the little mare. Well, more than that, for the stableman said she was with colt.

I heard this news of wolves in the village from an old storekeeper whom everyone calls "Popov." His full name is Stefan Pavel Popov. He has been a merchant in the village for over thirty years. He was a favorite of our young lady in the portrait. When she was a little girl, Popov was always giving her sweets and small toys whenever her father or I took her to Popov's general store. The merchant currently keeps this estate stocked with pork and other meats, as well as fruits and vegetables when they are in season.

Two days ago, I had driven one of the estate's wagons into the village to pick up provisions. As I drove the supply wagon through the streets, I noticed at one point that several men were washing what appeared to be dried blood from the left front wheel of a large coach. They were speaking in whispers, but I made out the word "wolves." Intrigued, I decided to visit Popov's store immediately, for I knew that if there had been any strange goings on in the village, old Stefan Popov would know and would be glad to tell.

As soon as I crossed his doorstep, I heard Popov say to several of his customers that the coach had stopped directly in front of his shop to allow the passengers to disembark. The old merchant said that one of the ladies, immediately upon leaving the coach, had thrown her arms skyward as if seeking God's intervention, and then fainted in the street. She was revived in just a few moments after the coach driver splashed cold water on her forehead. As she regained consciousness, her legs and arms flailed about wildly and with seeming abandon, much to her husband's embarrassment. Finally, she rose to her feet, helped by the steadying hand of her spouse, and they slowly walked home, for they were villagers themselves. The other travelers were strangers to the hamlet. Shaken by the wolf attack, they sought refuge in the inns or boarding houses of the village.

Old Popov told the story of the attack so well, with an animated face and many a flourish of his hands. He spoke with a slight lisp, which endeared him to the ladies. A small crowd had gathered around to listen and watch him gesticulate. I was among them. At one point in the tale, he paused, threw his head back, and gave a perfect imitation of a howling wolf. I laughed with the others, but the authentic sound unsettled a child who then began to cry. Popov gave the child a sweet from the shelf behind him and continued his story. Then, in describing the large wolf, he drew his lips back from his teeth and snarled most convincingly. For just an instant, his countenance was that of a wolf. At this, three men in the audience cheered and stamped their feet in approval. At the conclusion of his story, the storekeeper praised the courage of both the gelding and the brave driver who delivered all the passengers safely to the village. When he finished his account, the crowd applauded him, and several of the men clapped him on the back and shook his hand and made much of him. I'm sure that the next time he tells the story of the attack, he will enhance it with more wolf howls and perhaps the neighing of horses.

Oh yes, sir, I believe the depiction of the wolves is factual, for the heroic coach driver is the old storekeeper's nephew, a powerful and athletic young man, although he walks with a slight limp that he's had since childhood. He is nearly as tall as you are, sir, and is known throughout the village for his honesty and courage. Many in the village say that no other youth can surpass him in strength. I'm sure he gave a simple and true account of the wolf attack, for the young driver stammers and stutters when he speaks; therefore, he uses no more words than are needed.

But Popov and others in the village are known to exaggerate in telling their tales. They like to embellish their stories, sometimes with superstitions and often with delusions. If you sit drinking ale with them near a flickering stone fireplace with the wind howling outside in the cold, dark night, they will tell you old tales of men who could take the shape of wolves and wolves who, in an instant, could turn into men. They will speak of Vlad the Impaler, the second son of Vlad Dracul, a cruel young tyrant who, later in his life, came to be called "Dracula." I can see by the look in your eyes that you have heard of the villain and his deeds. He has been dead many centuries, but the villagers still tell of Vlad and his brutal harshness. Also, they will tell of women who can fly throughout the village and do all manner of sorcery in the name of the devil. They will speak of old graveyards with open coffins, and men and women who won't stay dead. They will speak of men and women who have crawled up from their graves to wander alone and lifeless through these mountains, looking for God knows what. The village storytellers say these undead creatures will stand side-by-side with wolves and howl with them in the dead of night. I grew up in the village, and I am steeped in the village's superstitions and stories, especially those about Vlad.

What's that, sir? About Vlad? What are the stories about the Impaler? You've no doubt heard, sir, that in the town square, there are three huge stones that were, according to legend, taken from Vlad the Impaler's castle. When the weather permits, the village entertains visitors who come to touch the stones and tell stories of Vlad. It is said that he appreciated fine art, and inside his castle were exquisite paintings and magnificent statuary that he had obtained through plunder or by purchase, for he enjoyed great wealth and power. He was a complex man who showed kindness to animals and children; however, his brutality toward his enemies, both real and alleged, was legendary.

Several in the village say he was a great leader and protected this land from invasion, but most say he was a cruel tyrant whose viciousness exceeded that of any man. Certainly his means of dispensing with his enemies by impaling their bodies with sharp stakes rivals the horror of crucifixion. Impalement insured suffering before death, and it is said that Vlad enjoyed walking among his impaled victims, listening to their moans as if listening to the music of a great orchestra. Vlad carried with him a large goblet half-filled with red wine. Legends say he sometimes intermingled the blood, dripping from the fingers and toes of his suspended victims, with the wine.

I have heard the elders of the village church say he was pure evil, and that is why the fly-lord, Beelzebub, second in command in Hell's hierarchy, gave him the dispensation of eternal life. Yes, sir, eternal life! Imagine, if you will, the blessings, or perhaps the curses, of eternal life. So, some in the village will say Vlad lives on, but I believe he is harmless dust, resting in some bejeweled coffin buried deep in the soil of these mountains. Dust to dust. Someday, sir, our flesh, blood and bones, will be nothing but dust. However, Vlad's legend lives on.

Sir, you'll have to speak up. Speak just a little louder, please. Forgive me. At my age, I don't hear so well. That's it, sir. Now I can understand you. And what a loud and deep voice you can muster!

Oh, you wish to hear a story! A story of Vlad! If you compel me, sir, I will tell you a story of the Impaler. But I must warn you, sir, I am long-winded, and like old Popov and the villagers, I tend to embellish my tales. My wife, bless her, is always telling me, "Get to the point, Husband! Get to the point!" More than once, she has boxed my ears in order to clear my head and move me more swiftly to the conclusion of a story.

Bear with me a moment, sir, while I gather my thoughts, which are spread amongst the clutter in my dusty old brain. My wife says my skull is full of cobwebs, and perhaps she is right. But if you will be patient with me, sir, and forgive my hyperbole, I will speak of the time when Vlad was a man of flesh and blood. There now, I've conjured up a tale of the Impaler.

It is said that in the olden times, when Vlad had dominion over this land and its people, he invited a dinner guest to his fortified castle. Save for the servants, the two men dined alone at a table that could have seated twenty. After a sumptuous dinner of roasted venison, Vlad took his guest into his vast flowering gardens, but he wanted to show his visitor more than just the hundreds of blooming roses. Among the vast number of growing lilacs were several of Vlad's enemies who had been impaled on sharp, pointed poles and stakes. Horses and pulleys were somehow used in the impalement, but I know not how. One newly impaled victim was still alive and moaning incoherently since the long stake exited through his mouth. One can only imagine, sir, where the ghastly penetration commenced. Nevertheless, the victim gurgled and garbled, spouting forth bloodied gibberish.

This behavior unsettled Vlad's dinner guest.

Vlad had seated himself and his dinner companion at a small table near the dying man who still writhed feebly on the stake. Crimson bubbles surrounded the poor creature's mouth and nostrils. Though his movements were, for the most part, involuntary, he seemed to be stretching a bloodied arm and hand with long, distended fingers toward Vlad. Then, with the hand mere inches away from the back of Vlad's dark head, the victim's arm would drop to his side, seemingly lifeless. The stake held him securely in place, making it impossible to reach

Vlad; however, after only a few seconds, the limb would rouse itself, and again the dying man would ineffectually reach toward his tormentor. He was, for all practical purposes, blind, for his eyelids had been sewn shut. His hand rose, stretched, reached, and fell limply again and again. The dinner guest had the uncomfortable feeling that the unfortunate man on the stake had stopped reaching for Vlad and had begun reaching for him.

Servants brought strawberry cakes and chilled milk to Vlad and his companion. The dessert was Vlad's favorite, according to legend, and he consumed many pieces of the cake and the other strawberry pastries that were placed before him and his guest. Untouched, a large piece of the strawberry dessert rested on a golden plate in front of Vlad's guest. Vlad gaily chatted about the weather, the songbirds, and his roses. As the two talked, Vlad ate very quickly and with enthusiasm. Soon, the red berry juice was dripping from the corners of Vlad's mouth. He wiped his lips clean with the white cuff of his linen shirt, but his thick mustache remained red, as if stained by blood.

Suddenly, there was a great exhalation of breath from behind Vlad. The impaled victim's eyelids ripped open, tearing the stitches and leaving his eyes wide open, looking skyward. Nothing but the whites of his eyes could be seen, for his eyes had rolled far back in their sockets. The pinioned body of the dying man shuddered, and then slipped several inches down the wooden stake, leaving a stain of gore. His suffering was over.

"May God rest his soul; may he find peace," said the dinner guest, staring intently at the corpse.

"Do you recognize him?" said Vlad, observing his guest closely as he stroked his red mustache.

"No," replied his companion. "But surely this man has suffered enough here on earth. Certainly a merciful God will grant him forgiveness, no matter what his crime."

"Those are the words of a Christian. Are you a Christian?" asked Vlad.

"Yes, I am, and a devout one."

"Tell me, my friend, do you believe in life after death?" asked Vlad.

"Yes, I do. I believe that shortly after my death, I will see my Savior in a better world."

"Your words give me comfort, old friend, for I fancy myself a Christian also but of a different sort. My God is more vengeful than yours. Sins are punished more than forgiven," said Vlad. He pointed to the fresh corpse impaled nearby on a blood-red stake as if to illustrate his philosophy.

Other stakes in the garden held corpses of both men and women in various stages of dissolution. One stake held the cadaver of a corpulent woman who had been disemboweled prior to being impaled, no doubt for committing adultery or some other forbidden act. Her remains produced a vile stench. Flies buzzed and whined in and out of her open abdominal wound, feeding, mating, and laying eggs. The odor from her corpse and the older corpses was overwhelming, and Vlad's guest complained bitterly about the fetid smell, holding a lace handkerchief to his nose.

"The odor of rotting flesh and the constant buzzing of these black flies—how can you bear it!" cried the dinner guest, clapping his hands against his ears. "My breath is taken from me! My skin crawls! Let us go inside at once and escape this foul air!"

Vlad smiled as a soft wind ruffled his thick, dark hair. A quick wave of his wrist brought seven of his guards rushing toward him. They stood before him and awaited his orders. Rising from the table, Vlad placed his hand on the shoulder of a tall young man to whom Vlad had given the rank of captain. The young captain's coat was a resplendent blue with gold brocade at his cuffs and collar. Vlad whispered in the captain's ear.

The officer immediately dispatched several of his men to fetch an unusually long stake. One guardsman held the bridles of two large horses and walked between them, leading the white steeds into the garden. A stake nearly thirty feet in length was procured, and one of Vlad's men began sharpening one end of the stake. One of the horses began to scrape at the ground with a huge hoof; both horses flicked their tails nervously. Apprehension spread across the countenance of the dinner guest. His hands trembled, and his breath came in gasps. He stared at Vlad with wide eyes, for he was beginning to comprehend his own fate.

The Impaler then told his guest he recently had learned of certain foul treacheries against his domain and his authority—disloyalties so great and so hateful that death, and a painful death at that, was the only recourse. Vlad then accused his dinner guest of being the perpetrator of these numerous treasons against him.

"But you did not act alone against me, did you?" Vlad smiled as he raised his hand and pointed to the fresh corpse on the stake. "Look more closely at the impaled traitor, for death has softened and relaxed his features that were moments ago twisted in a grimace of pain." Vlad picked up a pitcher of water from the table and threw its contents into the face of the slowly stiffening corpse. The water washed gore and blood from the victim's face, leaving a much cleaner countenance.

"My God! It is my brother!" cried the dinner guest, rising from his chair. The young captain, grabbing Vlad's guest by the shoulders, forced him back down into his chair. The dinner guest placed his head in his hands and began to weep.

"Yes, he is your brother, and he has confessed all, hoping that a confession might yield him some measure of mercy. I laughed at him, of course. I have no mercy for traitors. And now, I fear that you, his fellow conspirator, must join him in death, but first, the pain. Yes, before your death, you must endure the pain. When you die, you will find yourself in a better world. You said so yourself. Oh, one more thing, my old friend. A few moments ago, you complained about the stench here in my garden. I rather like the smell, but I have heard your complaint and I shall try to remedy the situation. Also, as a fellow Christian, I'm delighted to hasten your journey to the other world, the land of many mansions. But not too fast, first you must experience the suffering. My goodness, we're both shaking. Your tremors come from dread. Mine from anticipation!"

Vlad told his shivering victim that since they were once boyhood friends and close companions, he would be impaled on the longest stake available. And so he was impaled and lifted twenty feet into the air. He suffered a prolonged and terrible death, as did his brother. He was, however, placed high above the other decomposing victims, where the stench of death was much reduced and sometimes carried away completely by the frequent breezes which spread the sweet scent of blooming roses from Vlad's nearby garden.

It was in this fashion that Vlad the Impaler showed both his abnormal cruelty and his unique kindness.

Well thank you, sir. I am pleased that you enjoyed my tale. Perhaps I have not strayed so far from the village myths and the tales of the village storytellers. My story of Vlad was embellished a bit. I fear hyperbole is one of my faults. I could not resist. You see, sir, there was no brother and no rose garden. The rest, according to legend, is true.

The story I just told you, sir, contrasts with the stories told in the village in this way: my character was a flesh-and-blood tyrant. Truly, he was above the law; however, he was a mortal man. His cruelty died with him. The tales that come from the village concerning Vlad make him a creature that lives on, century after century, an evil entity who still walks the streets of the village, doing as he pleases. Pure superstition, I tell you. Vlad is the very foundation of the villagers' delusions and imaginings, and stories of him and his creatures abound. I heard them all as a youth. The peasants in the village can't let go of Vlad and his stories.

You would like to hear more about Vlad, sir? Very well. Mind you, these are tales I've heard in the village. There are stories of a man who had been beheaded by Vlad centuries ago, and yet he still makes his way through the forests, feeling his way from tree to tree. The witches who fly over roofs and chimneys during the night and scream obscenities at the good women below are said to be Vlad's concubines. The man-wolves, who can convert from man to beast then back again in an instant, protect Vlad, as do the pure wolves of the forest. The corpse walkers—some of whom have long, broken stakes sticking through their ribs—are his slaves, and they continue to suffer terrible cruelties at his hands. Vlad himself hovers like an incubus over sleeping women. Sometimes, I'm told, he descends to lie with a woman and leave her with child. The children that Vlad is said to have spawned always have some singular deformity—a cleft palate, a blind eye, lameness, webbed hands, or an abnormally large head. One poor infant was said to have been born with all these abnormalities, but her labored breathing ceased only an hour after her birth. If these strange children survive the cruelties of their childhood peers, they are treated with deference and respect in the village, for the Impaler and his children are greatly feared.

All this about Vlad, I have heard from early childhood. Now I stand before you as a bent old man repeating the myths.

I tell you, sir, that what I have *heard* is not what I *believe*. No, I believe not a whit of it. You are a gentleman, sir, and I, for my own part, have read many books, thanks to old Sattran and his library. Although I am of a low station in life, I consider myself a literate man. You have, no doubt, put away the superstitions of your youth, just as I have discarded the delusions of the village. I believe not in flying witches, man-wolves, or corpse-walkers. I walk in the forest with no fear of the headless creature. I do, however, believe that Vlad existed centuries ago as a mortal man of flesh and blood, but I do not believe he continues to walk among us, exerting power over creatures such as witches, corpses, and wolves.

Yes, as you have, sir, I have put away my superstitions. There is evil enough in this world, and evil feeds on superstition. Our superstitions make it more difficult to deal with the real problems in our lives.

The wolves, however, are not products of fantasy. They are real enough. They are famished and, therefore, are very dangerous. Some of the wolves are almost hairless, nothing more than skin, bones, and teeth. I pity them.

Yes, sir. That's right. It is tragic, and this starvation is a result of the poachers who live in the village and their limitless, interminable greed. This great estate includes vast tracts of forested land, and the land was once a haven for deer. Both the deer and the wolves prospered, growing fat and sleek. To his credit, the old master, Petru, opened his lands, all his lands, to hunters during the month of October. He bade them to stock up with venison for the coming winter. Many deer were slain by the hunters during the month, but the balance between wolf and deer remained. When November came, Sattran forbade hunting on his land. He announced that any man caught on his land and in possession of a slain deer after the month of October would be severely punished.

Truly, sir, old Sattran could stop the deer thieves when he was alive.

***

This day marks a tragic anniversary of the old master's death. I cannot talk about his death without tears spilling from my eyes. My voice is cracking now, for he was like a father to me, sir. Perhaps, tomorrow, I can tell you more about the old master and how he died. But today, I prefer to talk about the way he lived.

He was a vigorous man, sir, and he relished defending his lands. He and his riders hunted poachers for sport. If they caught an unfortunate man with a slain deer, the old master climbed down from his horse and surveyed the size of the deer. If a large deer had been killed, the old man would use his heavy staff to break the poacher's arm just above the wrist. Sometimes, especially if he had been drinking, he ordered the poacher's collarbone to be broken, thinking the injury would be more painful and take longer to heal. If the deer were small, perhaps a yearling doe, the old master had his men break the poacher's thumb. If the poacher cursed or called out to God in any fashion during his ordeal, his other thumb or another finger would be broken. The old master was, in his fashion, a very religious man. In all my years of service, I never heard him curse, and he was very kind to me.

The old master's daughter—yes, the lady in the portrait—witnessed her father mete out punishment one afternoon in early November. Justina was fourteen years old at the time, as I recall. She was riding her pony,

Ribbons, on the old forest road when she came upon her father and two men holding a young poacher with his arms pinioned behind him. The young man himself could not have been more than thirteen or fourteen. He was stripped to the waist and was loudly cursing his captors. The young man's punishment had begun. She observed dispassionately for a few moments and then, when the young man screamed, she turned her pony around and galloped back to the great house. I don't know what the young mistress saw, but she cried all afternoon and did not come out of her room for the evening meal.

The poaching of deer began in earnest after old Sattran's death. The poachers knew the old man could not reach them from the grave. The villagers developed a taste for venison, and the poachers knew the young mistress of the house and lands would do nothing to stop their hunts. The entire village had heard of her soft heart and kindness. After the death of her father, the lady in the portrait would not hear of any punishment that she considered cruel, so the poachers soon learned they had a free hand to slay the deer. They did so with a vengeance. The deer were slaughtered by the hundreds and not always for meat. Antlers decorated the taverns and many houses in the village. I have seen rotting, fly-infested deer carcasses in the forest with just the antlers chopped away.

Now the deer are almost gone, for the poachers and wolves have decimated their herds. The wolves must nowadays rely on rabbits and forest mice for food, but their hunger, once assuaged by the deer, now seems insatiable. At night, near the village and even inside the village, wolves attack livestock—hogs, goats, and chickens, for the most part—but they also take cattle and horses. Piglets and calves are especially vulnerable. Wolves, like humans, have a liking for pork and beef, sir. I'm told that even the dogs and cats are not safe.

A child? Taken by the wolves? I think not, sir. Surely I would've heard of it. It's just more village gossip and exaggeration. You mustn't believe everything you hear in the village.

No, sir. Someone has given you false information. Indeed, I've heard the rumors spread by the local gossips. May I give you an example? The villagers say there is a terrible painting hidden somewhere within these walls. The specter in the portrait is said to wear a gown painted scarlet with blood. It is said to be the work of the young mistress, a self-portrait, painted during the dark days when she fought to maintain her sanity. Yes, I have heard that the portrait is always turned to the wall, and that if a person turns the portrait from the wall and looks upon it, he is blinded by the horror of it. Untrue!

I've spoken of the exaggeration, the hyperbole contained in the gossip from the village. Let me give you another example, sir. As I noted earlier, I grew up in the village. When I was a small child, just old enough to want to wander and explore, I longed to venture into the forest. My mother, however, told me to avoid the forest at all costs. She said I might encounter the old man whose terrible hunger drove him to swallow his own head. She said he was always looking for a nice, young head to replace the one he had swallowed.

You laugh, sir, and so do I now, but as a child, I was afraid of meeting the headless man. Because of him, I never wandered far into the forest. I tried to imagine what he might look like, and the image I created in my child's mind evoked more than one nightmare. My brother was six and I was five when Mother warned us about "The Swallower." That's the name we children gave the creature. My brother and I would walk to the edge of the forest and stare into the dense trees and plants. A passing shadow or snapping twig sent us scurrying home and into our mother's arms.

I believe it was my brother, not I, who gave the unfortunate headless man his name. As we got older, my brother and I made up stories about The Swallower to tease and frighten our younger sister. We even dressed up as how we imagined The Swallower looked and staggered around outside her window. With his face shrouded by blankets and rags, my brother sat atop my shoulders, for even though he was older, I was the larger brother. We tapped on her window and made gurgling sounds. When our sister came to the window and screamed, we toppled over onto the ground in fits of laughter. Afterward, Mother beat us until we were black and blue, so we never pretended to be The Swallower again. I see that I have brought a smile to your face, sir.

The evil painting of which the villagers speak is no more real than The Swallower. I have been all over this estate and in every room of the great house. I can promise you that no such painting exists. The only kernel of truth is that the young mistress battled madness almost daily during the last years of her life.

I can assure you, sir, that the portrait you see here is the only one of Mistress Justina. It was painted several years before her death. And was she not beautiful, sir? The artist has made her live again on that canvas. Her china-blue eyes shine just as before. Her broad, smooth forehead indicates a great intelligence. Her fair skin and auburn hair seem flushed with life. And I've been kissed on the cheek many times by those perfect lips, her way of showing thanks for some small kindness rendered. And note the somber and contrasting colors he chose for the background, sir, and the delicate perfection of the small, red rose in her right hand. The hand itself is so graceful and lifelike. It's almost as if she could reach from the canvas and touch you.

Yes, she was of medium stature and well-formed, her voice was musical and soft, and she was very articulate in her speech. If she turned her gaze upon you in conversation or from across the dining table, she made you feel as if you were the only person in her world. I miss her, sir. She was like a daughter to me.

Why did she not smile for the portrait? Is that what you asked? Excuse these old ears. I, as I've said before, don't hear as well as I should. I've had deafness in my left ear since birth. My wife sometimes has to shout at me to make me understand. To tell the truth, sir, the mistress did not often smile; indeed, there have been few smiles in this house. They came so seldom from our lady in the portrait that they were treasured and revered.

True, it would seem that one so beautiful and born to great wealth should have reason enough to smile; however, the portrait shows only her beauty and hides the reason for her melancholy expression. You will note in the painting, sir, that while the right arm and hand are visible, the left arm, including the hand, is completely covered by the thick, gray veil. Under that shroud, sir, rests the reason for the sadness that lingers in the eyes of the lady in the portrait. The veil covers the left arm, not by chance, sir. Not by chance.

That hidden limb was grotesquely deformed. How can I describe that veiled arm? I've seen it often enough. Though she always tried to hide it under her clothing, it would slither out from under its covering, exposing itself to all. The appendage made my flesh crawl. It was like the limb of some reptilian creature except for a few random patches of wiry hair. The skin that covered the arm was snowy white and had a coarse and abrasive texture. Thick, dark hair grew on the wrist, and folds of scaly skin hung from the forearm. On the inner wrist, about two inches above the palm, conjoined arteries and veins tangled, forming a purple swelling under the skin. The small, inflamed lump pulsed rhythmically. The pale left hand itself, sir, was large and hairless with blue veined fingers, and the blackened nails of the hand were round and pointed at the tips like a claw or a talon. In the middle of the palm was what appeared to be an open wound. The slit, opening and closing as if gasping for air, oozed not blood but a clear, bubbling liquid like saliva. The knuckles were swollen and prematurely arthritic. Between the hand's forefinger and thumb, there was a split in the skin, and within the fleshy aperture, there was what appeared to be a dull blue clouded eye. I know it could not have been an eye and yet ....

Well, my wife, who saw the orb several times when the hand was uncovered, thought it was some kind of malignant growth or hateful tumor. "You don't see eyes growin' out of hands, Husband, and that's a fact," she said to me. "Like as not, it's the cancer growin' on her hand. It'll spread all over her, just as it spread all over my father, unless a doctor cuts it out. But it's not my place to give our lady medical advice. I'll not say a word to her about it."

My wife's father had died of cancer from a mole he'd had since childhood. Located under his right eye, the mole turned black as night and began to spread quickly across his cheek. Then a cancerous spot appeared in his eye, first in the eye nearest the mole and then in the other. The growing malignancy blinded him in a matter of days, then it fled to the skin around his lips. His lips blackened, dried, and then fell away from his mouth, leaving him with a constant skeletal smile; and when the corruption reached his tongue, he found himself unable to speak or taste food. Finally, the cancer reached his lungs. He began coughing up dark, thick blood. Within a year after he found that darkening mole beginning its growth on his cheek, he was dead.

My wife, his only daughter, cried almost continually for a fortnight, but then it was over. Her eyes were red and swollen, but they were dry. She is a hardy soul and plainspoken.

"I've no more tears to shed," she said one day. "My father was a good man, and he had a good life. I've no more tears to shed for him, though I loved him dearly. He is dead and buried. When he could still talk, he asked only that the family bury him deep so the wolves could not get at him. There is no more I can do for him. He rests deep under the sod. I shall spend more time helpin' the young mistress now. Lord knows she needs my help, poor girl that she is, livin' with that useless arm."

The mistress had no feeling in that arm, sir, and no power of movement. Well, I say no power of movement, but to be more precise, sir, I should say no power of *controlled* movement. In truth, the arm, if it could be called an arm, did move in spasmodic contractions, causing the appendage to flail and thrash about uncontrollably at times.

The spasms, though rare when Justina was a child, increased in frequency when the mistress became a young woman. These outbreaks often occurred at the most inopportune moments for the mistress, and I have seen her retire many times to her bedroom because of convulsions in that limb. The flailing member was an embarrassment to her, sir. Once, while dining with guests, a sudden spasm of the limb caused the arm to crash into the mistress's china and wineglass, leaving a severe cut just above the wrist. Black blood streamed from the wound and almost instantly coagulated in the dark hair that encircled the wrist. Some of the blood spilled onto the table and arm of one chair. There were just a few droplets on the floor.

Our good mistress rose from her chair and cried out, "Clumsy fool!" Then she laughed most surprisingly, sir, for she felt no pain, although the wound was terrible. A shard of glass, fully two inches long, remained embedded in her forearm. She excused herself and immediately left the table. She returned an hour later to bid her guests goodbye and tell them she felt well. The arm, covered by bandages, remained still during the farewells, but that was the last time the mistress entertained guests. And as for the wound, it healed quickly and left no scar on the translucent scales of her lower arm.

It was my wife who cleaned the dried blood from the table, chair, and floor after the guests had left. She maintained that there was a rancid stench that emanated from the blood stains. The rank smell stayed in the room for days. The mistress had fresh roses fetched from the village and placed at the center of the dining table. The windows in the room were flung open to allow fresh air inside. In a matter of days, the disgusting odor subsided.

The lifelong torment that arm caused her, sir, you could not comprehend. She was around age ten when the teasing began. A certain cruelty manifested itself in the hearts of her playfellows, both boys and girls. One handsome young lad of eleven was particularly vicious in his remarks about her misshapen hand. His hurtful words cut her to the quick, for he had been her favorite. Witty and charming with an intelligence that matched her own, the lad began teasing Justina about her deformity. Soon, the other children joined in. And so she was taunted as a child by her playmates, and when she matured and became a young lady, the beauty of her face was no match for the grotesqueness of her abnormality. Word of her disfigurement spread quickly among the wealthy young men of courting age. She had no suitors, but she knew the reason. She was reminded of it each time she looked down at her hands, one perfect and one terrible. She grew to loathe that appendage as one learns to hate an enemy, and as her hate grew and festered inside her brain, her mind weakened, her grasp of reality loosened.

Her once stately character began to decay and crumble as the years passed. She became more and more of a recluse. As she moved about the house, she sought out darkened corners and shadowy places. We who loved her shared her torment and tried to comfort her as best we could. My wife has shed many tears for the mistress, for my spouse's exterior sternness belies a soft heart.

Yes, my wife works here also. She has worked for the estate longer than I. She came to work in the kitchen at the age of sixteen. Once, the old master, Sattran, caught the two of us kissing in a closet. He threw the closet door open and saw our embrace ... and our embarrassment.

"Here, here, indeed! What have we here? Does it take two to clean out such a small closet! And let us open the door wider so that there can be more light inside. Well, the closet looks clean enough. Step out, young man. Step out, young lady. Ah, I can see that you two must've been working hard, for your faces are flushed and you perspire," said old Sattran, throwing his head back and laughing. We laughed along with him, for we were young and had just commenced falling in love.

"Mark my words, there will be a wedding in this house within a year. We shall open the great hall and invite the whole village to the nuptials. The expense shall be my own," he said. He slapped my back so hard that I staggered forward a few steps. He took Mary's hand and kissed it. She smiled radiantly.

The old master was true to his word about having our nuptials in his home, and so we were married at an early age, both of us still children really. I tried to pay him back some of the money, for he spared no expense at our wedding. He would have none of it.

Are you married, sir? No? Well, I recommend marriage. You should find yourself a wife. Man was not meant to live alone.

My wife and I now live in a small cottage behind the great house. We were pleased to learn that in her will, our young mistress left us the right to live in the cottage until our deaths. Yes, she appreciated the efforts my wife and I made to brighten even her darkest days.

When the lady in the portrait was a baby, and I saw her shortly after her birth, she seemed perfect at first glance. She wriggled and cried like a normal newborn as the doctor wiped the birth blood from her pink skin. The little hand, the left one that was to grow so gruesome, seemed almost identical to the right hand, except for the nails, sir. The nails on the infant's left hand were long, white, sharp as tiny needles, and rounded at the tips. In her second week of life, the nails began to blacken and harden. My wife, who had become the infant's nurse, tried to clip the sharp nails back, but they grew so quickly.

My wife and I have served in this house for more than fifty years. Think of it, sir, a half century, working within these cold stone walls. Some would say a few years too many. At any rate, my father sent me to serve in this house because, at the time, there was little work for me in the village. I worked in the stables for over a year. One of the older house servants died, and on that very day, I was moved into this mansion to serve here. I slept my first night in the dead servant's bed while his corpse, waiting for burial, rested on the bench outside my door. I was affrighted the entire night. I half expected him, at some dark hour, to push me aside and reclaim his bed. I can tell you, sir, I got little sleep.

The master of the house learned I could read within weeks of my house employment, and he opened up his vast library to me. He suggested books I should read, and he took the time to discuss them with me after I had read them. He introduced me to Greek and Roman mythology. I was only eighteen at the time, and I read voraciously. I studied the old myths and legends that still flourish in these Carpathian Mountains. If I came upon a word I did not understand, the old master helped me to comprehend the meaning by using the context of the word. He taught me to speak properly, although I sometimes stumble with words as you may have noticed.

What I know of the world, I learned from old Sattran and his books, for I have never seen a city. I've spent my whole life either in the village or on this great estate. In my opinion, Petru Sattran was a great man. He was a thoughtful man who successfully managed this estate. He loved his much younger wife and his little daughter more than anything in the world.

When the mistress was a child of five, sir, I was chosen to assist her with her reading lessons. I was very proud. Indeed, I was delighted and honored. I helped her as best I could. In addition to being a beautiful child, she was also very bright and caught on very quickly. She was such a cheerful and active little girl. She was constantly being chided for running down the halls and up the stairs of this immense house. She smiled and laughed and was full of mischief. And, somehow, the deformed hand was less noticeable when she was a child. In those days, one had to take two looks to discover that the little girl's left hand was different from the right. At five or six, she had several friends and playmates who adored her and paid little, if any, attention to her deformity. Of course, that changed as the years passed.

The child's mother? Sir, I thought I told you of her death earlier, but perhaps it was another visitor. My mind gets muddled at times. We've had so many visitors since everything in this house is for sale. Many possessions have been sold already. The house has seemed so empty since Justina's death, and each day, more and more of her belongings are carted away ....

I wish ... She was so ....

Forgive me, where was I? Oh yes, the young mistress's mother died three days after giving birth. The blood flowing from her womb could not be staunched. The village doctor said he'd never seen anything like the hemorrhaging. Another doctor from the city, a surgeon of some renown, was summoned to this great house. He arrived at dawn on the second day, but his efforts were useless. The bleeding continued. The poor woman was in and out of consciousness. My wife was with her on her last day. They talked, read the Bible, and prayed together, and in the end, she died peacefully with the babe still cuddled in her arms.

After the death of his wife, old Sattran was a broken man. He did not live in this great house, sir; rather, he haunted the large rooms and wide halls. Once a robust man, he grew increasingly gaunt and feeble. He smiled only in the presence of his daughter.

One strange thing happened on the night of Lady Sattran's death. There was a loud knock on the door, and my wife rushed to answer it, thinking it might be another doctor summoned too late to save the dying mother. Upon opening the door, she encountered a tall, dark man standing in the dense fog, for the clouds were low and it was raining. He was well-dressed and had the air of a gentleman.

"Does the child still live?" he asked. My wife replied in the affirmative. "Then all is well," he said. He smiled, then turned and disappeared into the mist. I remember how my wife thought it peculiar that she heard no footsteps as he descended the stone steps of the mansion.

As I mentioned earlier, the young mistress's understanding of reality weakened with the passing years. Long before her death, her madness was evident. She began saying and doing inexplicable things. For example, she once stood in front of this portrait and asked, "Who is that wretched woman? She's terribly ugly, whoever she is!"

"Mistress, the portrait is of you. It is beautiful and so are you," I said.

"Nonsense! It should be taken down and burned!" she cried. "Each time I look at it, the strange woman's face becomes more hideous. Her awful eyes follow me about the hall. If you and the other servants weren't so curiously fond of the portrait, I would have had it destroyed long ago!" She turned to me and pointed to the portrait. "You have always loved the little princess slut more than me. Confess! It is she in the painting whom you love!"

"Mistress, the lady in the portrait is you. You and she are one in the same."

"You're mistaken. She and I are different, unbelievably different, as you will learn in the days to come."

With that, she strode down the hall toward her bedchamber. The fingers of her left hand were bent but spread wide, displaying distended veins, blackened nails, and that strange orb that bulged between the forefinger and thumb. Inflamed knuckles cracked as the thumb and fingers straightened. The long fingers began to slowly curl inward, and then the hand tightened into a taut fist, turgid and stiff.

She began giggling like a silly schoolgirl as she opened her bedroom door. She stood in the doorway for a moment, looking back at me. Using her good hand, she grasped her misshapen hand by its hairy wrist, raising its clenched fist to her lips. Her tongue flicked out, licking and kissing a swollen knuckle. Then she, looking back at me all the while, slowly withdrew into the shadows of her bedroom and softly closed the door. It was shameful, sir. I have never seen a woman act in such a manner. She stayed in her bedroom for two full days. My wife entered only to bring her food and empty the chamber pot.

On another day, at noontime ... yes, it was noontime, for I recall that the kitchen servants were busy preparing the midday meal. There were many other servants in the dining hall. Some were cleaning the large windows; several men from the stable and the gardener were repairing a portion of the stone floor near the door that opened to the gardens outside. Yes, it was that day at noon that something dreadfully embarrassing and even more shameful happened.

A storm was brewing outside, for I remember the thunder and the darkening skies. The wind howled over the roof, and lightning flashed in the distance. Several servants who were working in the garden rushed inside to avoid the pelting rain. It soon became dark, and my wife began lighting the candles on the large dining table.

The mistress entered the grand hall, wearing nothing but a white robe. She cast it aside and stood naked in the corner for all to see. The quivering light of candles played across her body. Her lips were painted blood red, as were her nails on her right hand and both feet. Her knees were slightly bent and her legs were held open. Her good arm was braced on the windowsill. The twisted, monstrous arm lay across her left breast, and then it reached down, trembling and shuddering between her thighs.

She was pleasuring herself, sir, or so it seemed to the servants who had gathered about. The servants stood as if frozen. They could not tear their eyes from her. She leered back at them and ran her pink tongue across her scarlet lips, touching her sharp upper teeth. Her face was flushed, as were her shoulders and neck. Her brow was furrowed with deep wrinkles. Her breathing became a frenzy of rasping gasps. Droplets of perspiration formed between her breasts. Her glittering eyes darted about the room until she locked eyes with a young servant, a tall and muscular stable boy who was no more than seventeen. Her gaze transfixed the young man. He stood shivering with mouth agape. Moaning, he lowered his hand to his groin.

Suddenly, her hips thrust forward rhythmically, her back arched, her body convulsed, and she shrieked in her ecstasy. The wailing continued as she threw her head back until one could only see the whites of her eyes. The sound that came from her throat was the guttural sound of an animal.

I saw her robe resting on the floor and threw it over her, concealing her nakedness. Taking her by the shoulders, I walked her back to her bedroom. Wrapped in the large robe, she shuddered and began to cry pitifully like a child. She entered the bedroom, then turned and thanked me. I stood outside the closed door for many minutes, listening to her weep. Then there was silence, and I knew she had fallen asleep.

The next morning, I found her in the sunlit pantry, sitting cross-legged on the floor. Birds were singing outside and, in the distance, I heard the barking of a dog. The mistress was wearing a black silk robe that I had not seen before, and little else. The vile left arm rested slightly behind her as if avoiding the sunlight. She sat under a bright window with buzzing flies striking at the window pane again and again, trying mindlessly to escape her and her nimble fingers. On the floor in front of her were at least twenty buzzing flies unable to fly. Each fly was missing a single wing, the left one. She abruptly reached upward toward the window and snatched a large fly. In the deft fingers of her right hand, the mistress held up the frantically struggling insect. She brought the insect to her mouth, and with her teeth, she tore away a single wing. She spat out the wing and threw the crippled fly to the floor where it joined its wounded, earthbound fellows, buzzing and skittering about on the stone floor, making zigzag patterns.

"Care to join me?" she asked, looking up at me. "I know it's terribly wicked to wound them like this, to take away their gift of flight, but it gives me such a pleasurable feeling of depravity. Each torn wing yields a tiny droplet of blood that is wonderfully sweet. Look at them, buzzing and spinning on the floor, quite out of control and helpless. But I feel no pity for them. They are such nasty, wretched little creatures, rather like … like me, don't you think?"

Suddenly, the lady's hideous left arm came to life and raised itself to the level of her eyes, then paused. The hand and wrist turned as if observing the skittering flies on the floor. A thin film covering the blue orb between her forefinger and her thumb retracted. The forearm began to sway from side to side. The closed fist reminded me of a drawing I had seen of a venomous snake, a cobra, sir. I believe the illustration was a representation of the king cobra, a creature native to a warm, faraway land that I shall never see.

The gnarled fingers of the terrible hand spread wide and stretched themselves, revealing the long, pointed nails. Then the hand, like the head of a serpent, struck instantly downward toward the floor and impaled five of the droning flies. The hand raised and thrust itself toward my face with the pinioned insects still wriggling and squirming, one speared fly on each of the lengthy, blackened nails.

"Am I not like Vlad, the evil one of olden days?" the young mistress whispered. Her smile was dreadful. "Behold my impaled prisoners. And does not Vlad the Impaler still walk the village streets in the black of night, shrouded by fog and rain? Does his spirit not haunt these halls, each of the bedrooms, and even the crypts of my parents below? Does he not howl with the wolves outside our windows? Are not the scarred, the lame, the disfigured people of the village his children? Am I not his child? Look at this ghastly arm and hand, and answer me truthfully, you old fool!"

Recoiling in horror, I ran headlong from the pantry and rushed down the hall. I stopped before the portrait, arrested by its beauty. I stood breathing heavily and stared at the painting for a long time, reminding myself of how wonderful the mistress used to be. I glanced down at my hands. They were growing numb and trembling. The numbness crept up both arms, and I found that I could no longer control them as they flapped about, sometimes striking the wall, sometimes striking the portrait itself. A great nausea flooded my soul. I began to retch uncontrollably. My good wife came to help me, and she supported me as I made my way to the hall's large chair with the crucifix hanging above it. She brought me several drafts of strong whiskey, which I drank gladly. The warmth of alcohol coursed through my veins, and I could again feel my hands.

Each day, sir, we waited to see what new horror would be exhibited. On some days, the mistress would scream and curse at that left limb, and since there was no feeling in the arm, she would abuse it terribly. Once, my wife found Justina in the master bedroom near the fireplace. She was thrusting her left arm into the midst of a crackling fire. My wife pulled her away from the huge hearth and saw that strange appendage, writhing in agony like a white snake. The dark hair around the wrist was singed and smoking. There was a stench in the room, the stench of burned flesh. We kept the windows opened for many days, and finally the vile odor left.

In the following days, sir, my wife and I noticed that the violent spasms in the mistress's wretched arm continued and worsened. We felt she was becoming a danger to herself. My wife and I began to sit just outside her chamber door until very late at night. We fancied ourselves her protectors, I suppose.

One night, from Justina's room, there were shouts and oaths directed at the appendage. The screaming went on late into the night until her rasping voice deepened and became … became almost masculine. Then the foul whispering began. I could make out some of the lewd words. It sounded almost as if there were two voices engaged in intimate conversation spiced with obscenities and vulgar suggestions. I heard a gruff, lengthy moan followed by a few breathless gasps and sharp cries. Then there was a prolonged silence as the mistress at last slept.

The next morning, the mistress awakened haggard and tired. She suddenly began to look much older. Her hair grayed and grew long. Her once silky curls became brittle, and her teeth began to darken. Deep facial wrinkles formed, especially around her eyes and mouth. Folds of loose skin hung from her once smooth and supple neck. Oh, she was not at all like the woman in the portrait, sir. One had to look deep into her sad eyes to see any trace of our beloved mistress.

In the last few months of her life, she began a most ghastly nightly practice. With erect posture, she would stand and thrust her bare back against her bedroom wall. She ran her right hand through her hair until it was disheveled and flyaway. Her hair hovered around her head as if thousands of tiny spiders had woven gossamer webs around her scalp. Her aged, drowsy eyes were half-closed and heavy lidded. She flexed the muscles of her calves and thighs, which remained youthful and lithe. These contractions in her lower limbs seemed to arouse and then set into motion her terrible left hand, which began to rise, pausing only briefly to cup and caress her left breast.

Her left limb would then slither forward, shoulder high, along the walls and through the open doors, pulling her along behind it. Her arm and she slipped along the walls and across the doorways. She made her way from room to room. At times, she became exhausted and breathless, and the arm would coil on the mantle above the fireplace as she stood there looking in the mirror and resting. In a few minutes, the brief respite was over, and the skulking movements began yet again with quickened pace. This practice happened late at night, and often the mistress was completely nude. Even as her face aged, her lower body remained strong and supple. She upstretched her legs high as she stepped forward with pointed toes as if she were a ballerina performing some bizarre, erotic dance. All innocence disappeared from her face as she crept from room to room. Her eyes began to widen as she looked into each dark corner for something or someone. With an obscenely elongated tongue, she licked her scarlet lips and sharp teeth. Her constant leer was brazen and seductive, and her face was not the face of my mistress, sir. It was the face of a harlot, a common street prostitute. She laughed hideously as she left each darkened room. The appendage, sliding and rasping its scales along the walls, pulling our willing mistress along, avoided the lighted rooms and moved only toward darkness. She slinked along with flashing eyes and wildly flowing hair streaked with ghostly gray.

The mistress referred to the strange practice as "creeping." And she became more and more enamored of, if not addicted to, this behavior. She began creeping earlier and earlier in the afternoons, especially if the sun was hidden by storm clouds. Thunderstorms delighted her. When lightning flashes sent crazed shadows across the wall, the grotesque arm would stiffen and raise itself toward the ceiling, fist clenched. The mistress, or the creature that she had become, howled with a wide mouth in unbridled joy as the arm convulsed.

My wife, sir, who often acted as Mistress Justina's personal servant during the last year of her life, was brushing our young lady's hair last October as the mistress sat in front of her in the antique Brazov chair, gazing into the wide mirror. The mistress's hair, once so soft and smooth, was grizzled and brittle. My wife said it was difficult to pull the combs and brushes through the stiff, matted hair. She said to our lady, "You must go to bed early tonight, my dear. Lord knows you need your rest."

The mistress, however, grinned broadly and said, "Tonight there will be a full moon, and I'm sure we, the arm and I, will go creeping. It is much better to creep on moonlit nights than on cloudy nights when no shadows are cast on the walls. And with the full moon, the wolves shall howl beautifully tonight. It's so exciting to creep in the moonlight with the music of the wolves coming in through the open windows. Won't you come with us tonight, Mary? He said I might bring a guest someday, and creeping is the easiest thing to learn. It is so pleasing to feel the smooth, flat walls against your naked skin as you creep. I will show you how. He says we all have it in us, the desire to creep, that is. Won't you come?"

"No, by heaven, I shan't!" said my plainspoken wife. "This 'creepin',' as you call it, is from the devil. I shan't be part of it, Mistress, and I shall pray for you this very night. I shall pray for your soul."

The mistress's countenance changed. She took my wife's hand with her good right hand and squeezed it. Her eyes were pleading. She kissed my wife's hand and held it against her heart. "Yes," she said, "pray for my soul. Tonight and every night, pray for my soul." At these words, the mistress's left hand rose and covered her mouth tightly. The mistress turned and ran down the hall toward her bedroom. At the bedroom door, she paused and looked back at my wife. Using her right hand, she struggled to pull the larger left hand away from her mouth. At last, she thrust it away from her mouth so she could speak. Her eyes were frightened and welling with tears. "Promise me that you will pray for my soul every night, Mary. Swear that you will!"

"I swear before you and Almighty God that I will," promised my wife.

"God bless you," the mistress said as she disappeared into her bedroom. My wife found it odd that the bedroom door slammed shut with great force.

Three days later at breakfast, sir, we were all relieved to see the mistress was fully clothed and buttoned-up. She carried with her a large, heavy book, which she deposited on the table. The offending arm hung limp and motionless at her side.

Her eyes were clear and calm; her voice was gentle and soft. Her skin was so much smoother than it had been just the day before. It was as if the lady in the portrait had come back to us after being absent for many months. She ate with good appetite that morning, sir. I noticed that between bites and during conversation, she rested her good hand on the large, leather-bound book. Before leaving the table, she turned to my wife and said, "I want to thank you for praying for me. I know you did pray for me. I felt it. Your prayers have given me courage and strength."

"You're welcome, Mistress. I am but a plain, blunt woman, even when I pray. I asked the Almighty to hold your soul in the palm of His hand, and to protect you from the Evil One. I said the same prayer for your mother when you were just a baby. I shall remind our Lord again when I fall to my knees and bow my head tonight."

The mistress nodded to my wife and rose from the table. My wife helped the mistress put the weighty book under her good arm; and when it was secured, the lady in the portrait, who had miraculously returned to us, walked down the great hall toward the garden. When she passed her portrait, she stopped and regarded it. She placed the weighty book on a table near the portrait and then reached out her good hand and touched the rose in the painting. She was smiling, but her likeness, frozen on the canvas, remained solemn.

My wife grasped my arm as we were cleaning the breakfast table and said, "Husband, did you see the heavy book that she held? It was her mother's Bible. I have, at last, kept the promise I made to the dyin' woman many years ago. God have mercy on my soul, I almost forgot that sacred promise. I have never told you this, but I shall tell you now."

She released my arm and sat down at the table. She bade me sit down. She leaned forward and grasped my hands and held them as we were wont to do in our old courting days. Her eyes were earnest and her voice was calm. Her steady gaze captivated me. I could not look away.

My wife's words were plain and simple. I shall never forget them, sir.

"Husband, before she died, our young mistress's mother confessed to me that she had sinned with a man in the village. She and the old master had quarreled on the mornin' of that day, and she had taken the green carriage pulled by the speckled mare into town all by herself. She bought some flowers from a street merchant near the bakery. From the bakery, it was a short walk to the abbey where she had married the old master. Also within the walls of the old abbey were the graves of her father and mother. She was placin' flowers on her father's grave behind the village church. A pretty thing she must have been, still in her twenties. A tall, middle-aged man approached, dressed all in black except for a crimson shirt. She said he was olive-skinned; his black hair was flecked with gray. He spoke with a strange accent, and yet his words were beguilin' to her. As he spoke, he touched her hand and she did not pull away as any God-fearin' woman should have done.

"Husband, I blush to tell you the rest, but I feel that I must. He seized her by the shoulders and pulled her behind a large tombstone where he kissed her and touched her private parts until her arousal was complete. He had his way with her, and the mistress said she did not resist. They carried out their adulterous act in the very shadow of her father's gravestone. A week later, they met again at the old mill near the church, where they continued their unlawful affair. As she was gettin' dressed afterward, she turned and asked him when they could meet again. 'Never, for I have grown tired of you,' he said. Then he walked away, and she never saw him again. And I believe that was a blessin', to never see him again, I mean.

"The point of the story is this, Husband: she was never positive that the old master was truly the father of her baby. She confessed to me that the father could have been the dark stranger."

As you can imagine, sir, I was stunned to hear my wife speak of such things, and had I not already been seated, I would certainly have asked for a chair.

And yet, my wife continued in this fashion:

"Husband, the Bible in the mistress's hand this mornin' was a gift from her long-dead mother. Before she died, the young mistress's mother bade me to give her child that same Bible when she came to the age of understandin'. Also, she wrote a note and placed it inside the Bible. With all good intentions, I placed the Bible with the note tucked inside it in a large trunk at the foot of the bed in the master bedroom. God forgive me, I forgot all about it as the years passed. At the time, I was more concerned about findin' a wet nurse in the village for the baby. There, at the bottom of the wooden trunk, the Bible had remained for over twenty years, for I gave the Bible to our mistress just last night. I know not what it said, but the note she read brought tears to her eyes. With the message in her tremblin' right hand, she rose up from the chair beside the bed and ran toward me. She stood before me, and I held her close while she wept. 'My mother loved me,' Justina said between sobs. I told her that her mother caressed and nursed her until her dyin' breath. She seemed so surprised. 'I didn't know,' she said. It was as if someone had told her lies about her mother.

"Husband, I could feel the goodness flowin' back into her body—into her soul—as I held her good hand. The other hung limp at her side. A great softness and tenderness came over our mistress, and the wickedness that we have seen so many times left her. The coldness left her eyes, and they became warm and lovin', like a child's.

"She spoke but little of the substance of her mother's note, Husband. And I suppose the words from a dead mother to her livin' daughter were meant to be private. But she did share this with me. The note directed her to a certain passage in the Bible. The passage was from the New Testament. The mistress and I searched by candlelight for the words until we found them. Once found, with a tremblin' voice, the young mistress read the passage over and over again, so many times that I learned it by heart:

'If thine right eye offend thee, pluck it out, and cast it from thee: for it is profitable for thee that one of thy members should perish, and not that thy whole body should be cast into hell. And if thy right hand offend thee, cut it off, and cast it from thee: for it is profitable for thee that one of thy members should perish, and not that thy whole body should be cast into hell.'

"The young mistress said, 'My mother was so wise. And she is still watching over me! Don't you feel her presence, Mary? I feel that at any moment, she shall step forward from the shadows. God grant me the courage to follow her guidance.' I agreed with her, of course, but for the life of me, I didn't know what she meant. I keep goin' over it in my mind, Husband, but I still don't understand."

With that, sir, the conversation with my wife ended, for there were chores to do. And speaking of chores, sir, there is much work to be done here in the house this very night. The deceased mistress's young cousin, Alexandru, has put me in charge of the other servants because of my age and experience. There is much cleaning to be done from the attics to the vaults below, for we expect many visitors tomorrow. No doubt much gold will cross the young master's palm as relics and treasures are purchased and taken away forever.

Yes, sir, the portrait will fetch much gold. I wish you luck when the bidding begins.

Oh, one thing more that you may be interested in purchasing. There is a very ancient Bible from Italy over here, sir, on this table. May I show it to you? Here you are. Feel the leather of the cover and notice the artwork. Also, the crucifix that hangs on that wall is fashioned from gold and ....

No? Yes, sir, I'm sorry, now I understand. You are *only* interested in the portrait. Yes, of course, I shall return at once the Bible to the table. Place it *in* the table's drawer you say? Quite right, sir. The Bible could get damaged resting on the table. Now it is tucked away.

I see in your eyes that you want to learn more about our young mistress before you bid on her portrait. Tomorrow, sir, I shall tell you more of our beloved mistress and her death. For now, my wife calls me. I must assist her in the kitchen. Tomorrow, sir. I shall not forget. My pleasure, sir. Oh, look out the window. I believe your carriage is waiting for you. Goodnight.

***

Good afternoon, sir. I trust my wife greeted you at the door and told you I would be here in the stables. Yes, I had work to do this morning and still more this afternoon. Only two horses remain, a gelding and a mare, the rest having been sold. I agree, sir, the mare is a beauty.

Come with me to the far corner. Watch your step, sir, the floors are uneven and the light is poor.

Yes, another dark and dismal afternoon. Your cloak keeps you warm, does it not? Mine, while not so fine, does the same for me. Perhaps the sun will shine tomorrow. Ah, here we are. Notice the tools that hang on this wall—scythes, axes, and hammers. I wish to call your attention to this hatchet. Here, let me get it down from the wall. There now. Notice the stains on the blade. Try as we might, the stains cannot be removed. They are bloodstains, sir. That's right, bloodstains.

It was with this implement that our young mistress freed herself from that wretched arm. Yes, she performed the amputation here in this place in the dead of night. My wife and I and the other servants were asleep. When morning came, I found her body lying where you now stand. Not only was the arm, which gave her so much grief, severed just above the elbow, but the wrist and fingers were also chopped away. Our Justina died from loss of blood. I regarded her body and was struck by her countenance. Her face, with eyes closed, was peaceful as if she were dreaming. I tried to awaken her, but of course, I could not.

The fiendish arm by her side twitched in the throes of death. I struck the thing several times with a heavy shovel. Then I pinioned the limb with a sharp stake through its flesh. Afterward, it moved no more. I ran from the stables to fetch my wife and the other servants. Tears were shed by all. Many knelt to pray. It was the darkest day of my life, for I loved the young mistress as a father loves his daughter.

My wife took from her apron a note she had found in the young mistress's bedroom. It read, *Goodbye to all. Thank you for your many kindnesses. When you find me, offer up your prayers that I may at last find peace. Place garlic cloves around me in my coffin and spread salt in a circle round my grave as they did for the dead in the olden days. Bury my corpse deep, for I fear not only the prowling wolves, but also the cruel limb that gave me so much pain. I know not how it lives, but it is neither my flesh nor any part of me. For God's sake, do not put it in the coffin with me. I ask that you bury me deep, but put the cursed arm even deeper in the sod and far, far away from my resting place. May God bless you all.*

We obeyed her wishes.

Here, sir, is the sharp stake I used to halt the movement of the arm. See how it is tipped with a black blood stain. It is strange that you smile, for most who hear of our young lady's death are saddened. It may be that you have seen horrors greater than the one I have described.

Come closer and see the word I've carved upon this wooden stake. Yes, the word is "Revenge." I have carved another word on the other side. Come still nearer so that you may see it. That's right, sir. "Death" is etched in the wood.

And now I strike! *Uungh!* I thrust ... I push hard ... then harder ... I force the stake deep into your chest!

You cry out! Dear sir, you stagger, you clutch your bleeding chest. You cough up red spittle. Your bloodied hands grip the stake. Can you not breathe? Oh, sir, I fear you are dying.

Yes, I laugh for I know who you are. You are the Evil One. You are Vlad the Impaler. No more shall you walk the dark streets of our village. No more, while good wives sleep, shall you father their children—children who are born blind, lame, and disfigured. No more shall newborn babes be drowned because they are too horrible or are in too much pain to live. No longer shall you take the shape of a wolf and kill with your pack. No longer are you immortal. Like the thousands you slaughtered, you now taste the bitter cup of death.

Flesh falls from your body. Your eyes tumble from their sockets. Muscle and sinew wither. I see your white skull. Through your ribs, I see your impaled heart convulsing. Your bones clatter to the floor. My God! Your cloak holds heaps of dust. You, Vlad, are dust, nothing but dust.

But hark, my wife calls. I hear her words: "Husband, come quick! Make haste! The portrait, she smiles! It is a miracle from God! Our young mistress, Justina, in the portrait, she smiles! She smiles!"

MISS THORNE AND THE
TALKING BOARD

Spring sunshine came through Miss Thorne's bedroom window and crept up her bed. Sunbeams brightened her face, which was the only visible part of her body. The remainder of her form was hidden beneath a tattered bedspread. If a stranger had seen her at that moment, he would've noticed the angelic quality of her countenance in the morning light. Her gray hair, lit by sunbeams, was restored to its original golden hue, and her sharp features, softened by sleep, lacked the sternness with which she faced her English classes at Central Ashe High School. Miss Thorne's expression during sleep would discredit the general feeling among her students that she was a veritable terror, for even students with exceptional daring became meek and serene under her level gaze. Also, she was considered by some to be a county legend in that she left an indelible impression on her students.

"Remember Miss Thorne?" they would ask.

"Yes," would be the answer. "Who could forget her?"

Former students remembered her handwriting on the chalkboard, how she never raised her calm, precise voice in anger, and the classroom bulletin board on which Miss Thorne displayed assignments done by students who had earned a B+ or better.

Miss Thorne awakened. She stretched her arms toward the ceiling and said, "Good morning" to no one in particular, for she lived alone, without a dog or cat to provide companionship. For one year, she had kept a parakeet, but on a warm summer day, the bird escaped through an open window.

Her home was modest, as were the homes of her neighbors. There were no mansions in the small mountain town of Jefferson, North Carolina, in 1962. Her house was painted white with a gray, shingled roof. The windows had faded blue shutters held in place by rusty nails. Yesterday, working outside, she had mowed her greening yard with a push lawnmower. Inside, her furniture was plain and unexceptional except for a large bookcase which bulged with books. The floors were neatly swept, and two rugs, one in her bedroom and one in the living room, should have been replaced years ago.

In the corner of her bedroom was a secretary desk that had been given to her by her grandfather. On the wooden desk was a flat, black board. It was rather large, about twenty-two by fourteen inches, and imprinted in white across the board's dark surface were the numbers zero through nine, the twenty-six letters of the alphabet, and the words "Hello," "Goodbye," "Yes," and "No." At the top of the board, in the middle section, there was a picture of a partial skeleton displaying only a skull with a rib cage. Instead of arms, the skeleton had the spread wings of an eagle. At the bottom of the board, the winged skeleton was replicated but upside-down. On the left upper corner of the board, a bright, flaming, oval-shaped sun was depicted with a human face in its center. On the upper right corner, a quarter moon was shown with the profile of a human visage. Bright moon beams emanating from the face formed an oval design comparable to the sun's oval. In each of the bottom corners, a large hand with spread fingers rose from a turbulent sea with a human eye in each palm.

A small red piece of wood shaped like a heart rested on the board. There was a round hole in the wooden heart with a small, circular magnifying glass inserted there. The board was oiled so the wooden heart could be moved easily. The board itself was called a "spirit board" by some; others referred to it as a "talking board." The more common name for the board was the "Ouija board."

A visitor to Miss Thorne's home would've been surprised to see the Ouija board among her possessions. Most owners of such boards were considered to be superstitious, but her current and former students would've described Miss Thorne as being rational and realistic, not the least bit superstitious.

However, some irrational people thought the board had a dark side—that the dead could communicate with the living through the use of a Ouija board.

Miss Thorne rose from her bed, turned on her Philco radio which rested on her nightstand, and then walked to her bathroom where she turned on the shower. She held her hand under the spray to test its temperature. She began the oft-repeated routine that got her ready for the school day. This would be her last day with her students, the conclusion of her long teaching career.

From the bathroom, she heard her radio playing in the bedroom. The local radio station specialized in country-and-western music, but one young announcer, fresh out of the Navy, had been playing a series of military songs for morning listeners—"Anchors Aweigh," "the Marines' Hymn," and others. She enjoyed one Air Force song in particular. Miss Thorne's students would have been surprised to learn that she sang in the shower.

"They took the blue from the skies and a pretty girl's eyes and a touch of Old Glory too ...." Anyone with a trained ear would've determined that Miss Thorne was not a songstress, and that her choosing to pursue a teaching career, rather than a musical one, was wise.

Margaret Grace Thorne had been a teacher for forty years, first at Jefferson High School and then—after several of the county high schools had been consolidated—at Central Ashe High School. She had taught the mothers and fathers of most of the students who were to be in her English classes today. Miss Thorne seemed ageless. When her students pulled their parents' old yearbooks from bookshelves to laugh at their fathers' hairstyles and giggle at their mothers' skirts and dresses, they were confronted by the visage of Miss Thorne in the faculty pages. Her yearbook portrait stared at them. It was the same level gaze she used when they had failed to remember that it was Coleridge—not Wordsworth—who had written *The Rime of the Ancient Mariner,* or when they had forgotten to capitalize "Bible" in an essay, or had allowed sentence fragments to slip into their written book reports.

Her students were puzzled by the protectiveness their parents displayed toward Miss Thorne. Fathers and mothers were quick to reprimand their teenagers if they heard discussions of "old Thorny face" or "Grouchy Gracie" or any of the other nicknames Grace Thorne had accrued over the years. Students regarded the warm feelings their parents exhibited toward Miss Thorne as a slice of the vast separation that always divides generations.

There had been rumors of Miss Thorne's retirement for several years, but she seemed a permanent fixture at Central Ashe High School. That is, until last fall when she had announced at a faculty meeting her intentions. In her usual even tone, she said, "Principal Beardsley, fellow teachers, and other instructional staff, for personal reasons, I have decided to retire at the end of this school year."

***

The faculty, which included several of her former students, had sat in silence, not knowing what to say or do. Principal Clarence Beardsley, also one of Miss Thorne's former students, cleared his throat and abruptly ended the meeting. Bells rang, indicating the beginning of the school day. Teachers rushed to their classrooms, knowing a teacherless classroom was an invitation that occasioned student mischief.

Miss Thorne stood at her classroom door and greeted her first period students by name, making eye contact with each student. She had found that the simple procedure assisted in classroom discipline.

***

With the approval of the county school board, the local PTA, having learned of her impending retirement, had given a dinner in Miss Thorne's honor. It was announced in the local newspaper. A surprising number had indicated that they would attend, necessitating the use of the Central Ashe's gymnasium instead of the school's cafeteria. Bleachers were rolled back, providing more room, and cafeteria tables were moved to the gymnasium. Tabletops were softened by cotton tablecloths and decorated by jars of spring wildflowers. Middle-aged men and women in attendance saw, with a certain amount of pleasure, that Miss Thorne was the same as they remembered her, courteous but unemotional and efficient.

After the dinner—baked chicken, green beans, mashed potatoes, dinner rolls, with apple pie for dessert—the superintendent of schools made a long, rambling speech, much of which was about himself with a sprinkling of praise for Miss Thorne. On the other hand, Principal Clarence Beardsley had much to say about Miss Thorne, recalling his days in her English classroom and the last ten years as her principal. He ended by saying, "Miss Thorne, would you like to say a few words?"

Miss Thorne rose from her chair. No one noticed how she winced as she stepped toward the podium. She said,

"I want to thank each of you for your attendance. It has been my honor to know you and to have taught many of you. At the age of twelve, I decided to become a teacher. The decision was a result of my interactions with my own teachers. At eighteen, I earned a small scholarship which allowed me to attend Appalachian State Teachers College. I worked in the college library, and my parents, with their savings, paid for my tuition and my room and board. I was able, after securing a teaching position, to pay them back, albeit slowly. I've taught for forty years. I've reached the age of sixty-three, and it is time for me to go. Although I was very young when I decided to become a teacher, I've never regretted that decision. My students and my fellow educators have enhanced my career beyond measure, but as you know, tomorrow is my final day with my students. I still have three essays to grade and return. Also, I must make lesson plans for the last day of school. So, with a thankful heart, I bid you a goodnight and a fond farewell."

The audience gave Miss Thorne a standing ovation.

***

The morning after the honorary dinner, Miss Thorne found her usual parking place and parked her ten-year-old Chevrolet next to Principal Beardsley's shiny, new Ford station wagon. Resting in the passenger seat next to Miss Thorne was a shabby black briefcase. After locking her car, she, worn leather briefcase in hand, walked across the Central Ashe High School parking lot and into the school. It was 7:15. The school day would begin at eight o'clock.

Benjamin Grimes, the school janitor, greeted her as she entered her classroom. He was leaning on his broom. "Mornin', Miss Thorne. I can't believe this is yore last day. We're sure gonna miss you around here come next year and you ain't here. I left a ripe, red grocery-store apple on yore desk, a good-tastin' apple for the best teacher this ole school ever had."

"Thank you, Ben. I shall miss you very much."

"Things are changin', Miss Thorne. Next year, my granddaughter, Polly, is gonna be at this here school along with several other black young'uns. They don't have to go to the county school for coloreds no more. I wish you could be here to teach 'em, ma'am. Polly has dreams about goin' to college one day."

"I wish I could be here too. I'd love to meet your Polly, but it's time for me to go."

"One more thing. I reckon you recollect five years back, when you let me borrow three hunderd dollars to get my ole car's motor and transmission fixed. Well, I wanted to…."

"Think nothing of it, Ben. You paid me back promptly."

"No, ma'am, I didn't pay you back promptly. My tobacker crop failed, and I couldn't pay you back for *two* years. Durin' them two years, you didn't say nothin' about that money."

"You're a man of your word, Ben. I knew you would pay me back."

"I just wanted to thank you one more time, Miss Thorne, 'cause I couldn' borrow that money nowhere else. I tried the two banks in West Jefferson, the First

National and the Northwestern banks. The bank fellers wouldn't even listen to me. I tried to get a small advance on my monthly paycheck, but I didn't have no luck. You was the only one who trusted me to pay that money back. I ain't never gonna forget yore kindness."

"Your words warm my heart, Ben. I'll certainly miss your cheerfulness and your friendship. How is your sister, Elizabeth? I haven't seen her at church for several months."

"Sister Lizzie has quit the church, Miss Thorne. She's been gettin' into devilment. Folks say she is tryin' to be a witch and cast spells on folks. Last week, I seen her mumblin' words while standin' over her ole broom which was layin' on the ground. I said, 'Lizzie, what're you doin'?' She said, 'Castin' a spell so that this wore-out broom can stand up and commence flyin' around the farm.' I said, 'Lizzie, you done lost what's left of yore mind.' She told me I didn't know nothin' about nothin'. That ain't all. Last week, she got herself a spirit board— some folks call it a talkin' board—and started messin' with it. She said she was gonna use that board to talk with Grandpaw Hubert Grimes, and he's been dead for thirty years. My sister has done gone plumb crazy on us. The family is gonna disown her if she don't straighten up and quit messin' with that spirit board and tryin' to be a witch."

"I'm sorry to hear that, Ben. I'm fond of Elizabeth, and I hope to see her back at church soon."

"Maybe she'll go back to church, and maybe she won't. Well, I gotta tote this ole broom down to the lunchroom and commence sweepin'. Goodbye, Miss Thorne."

"Goodbye, Ben."

Miss Thorne seated herself at her desk and took from her briefcase twenty graded essays and placed them on her desk. A wave of weakness swept over her, and she closed her eyes. "This too shall pass," she whispered. Miss Thorne's dizzy spells had become more frequent.

Her physician had given her various tests and determined that nothing serious was wrong. He gave her advice on her diet, advised her to stay hydrated, and told her she should take a daily vitamin. "Try to get more exercise, Miss Thorne. Physical activity is very important for a person of your age. Teaching can be a sedentary occupation. Teachers are confined to their classrooms, and they spend hours sitting and grading papers at home. Your retirement should give you more time to get out of doors and walk. I want to see you again in a month. My secretary will make your appointment."

Miss Thorne noticed that in the upper section of her open briefcase, there was a calendar with the date for her next medical appointment neatly penciled in. She wondered if she should tell the doctor about the vivid dreams she'd been having. Since her dreams were pleasant and not nightmares, she decided she would not mention them.

Doctor Thorpe wouldn't understand anything— neither the talking board nor my dreams, she thought. *How could he understand how wonderful I feel while dreaming? No! He is a man, a man of science and medicine. He couldn't possibly believe in the power of the board. Perhaps a woman might understand. No! I must tell no one!*

Miss Thorne, dismissing her thoughts, walked to the back of her classroom and opened the windows. The sun, rising higher in the cloudless sky, was spreading warmth outside. Birds were warbling and flitting from tree to tree. Two robins were hopping around under an oak tree and busily extracting flesh-colored earthworms from the moist soil. Pink, blue, and yellow flowers were blooming around the campus. She turned from the windows and began straightening the rows of desks in her classroom. On one desk was a caricature of Miss Thorne, carved with a pocketknife. The drawing of Miss Thorne emphasized her large, brown eyes behind her glasses, her widow's peak, and her nose, with its length and nostrils greatly exaggerated.

Ah, there's a cartoonist in our midst, and not without talent. Who is our budding artist? she wondered.

Miss Thorne returned to her teacher's desk and sat down. She picked up her attendance book and turned it to the page that listed her freshman students, all thirty of them. Fortunately, her senior classes were more manageable with twenty students in each class. She scanned her seating chart and discovered that the freshman, Watson Weaver, was the young cartoonist in question. His father, Jacob Weaver, was the manager of Weaver's Funeral Home and Weaver Cemetery. With cash, Miss Thorne had purchased a burial plot from Mr. Weaver. For over a year, she had been saving money to buy her casket. She was surprised at the cost of even the simplest, unadorned casket. Like her parents, Miss Thorne didn't want to be a burden to anyone at the time of her death.

"It's so expensive to die," she had said. Mr. Weaver nodded in agreement. Then he grinned and said, "Our caskets come with a lifetime guarantee, Miss Thorne, and I have never heard a single complaint from our customers. Rest assured, dear lady, the Weaver Funeral Home will be the last to let you down."

Miss Thorne couldn't avoid laughing out loud. "Those are old jokes, Jacob. You should come up with some fresh material. Here's my final payment."

"Thank you, Miss Thorne. By the way, how's Watty doing in your English class?"

"Watson is doing well enough. Since the school year began, I've seen definite improvement in his composition skills."

Watson Weaver's father smiled.

***

Miss Thorne knew exactly what she would say to Watson Weaver as he left her classroom on this last day of school: "Watty, just today, while straightening our classroom's desks, I discovered your artistic talent. Already you're a fine cartoonist. I suggest that next year, you take a class with Mrs. Burns, our art teacher." Using a scrap sheet of paper, Miss Thorne scribbled a note to herself as a reminder to speak with Mrs. Burns about Watson.

A solitary burst of teenage excitement entered Miss Thorne's classroom. Melissa Underwood skipped into the room and stood breathless before Miss Thorne who remained seated. Precocious and inquisitive, Melissa often came up with probing and unexpected questions during class discussions of literature. Miss Thorne approved of Melissa's curious nature. Although no other student could be sure of it, Melissa Underwood was one of Miss Thorne's favorites.

Melissa held an envelope in her hand. "I got ... I *received* a letter, Miss Thorne! I've been accepted. I'll be a freshman at Wake Forest this fall. The school is giving me ... I mean ... I've earned a scholarship. Oh, I can't believe it!"

"I'm very happy for you, Melissa."

"I'll be the first in my family to go to college, and I couldn't have done it without you, Miss Thorne. In my interview on campus, the Dean of the School of Education referred several times to your letter of recommendation. Thank you! Thank you! Thank you so much for recommending me."

"You need not thank me. It was your hard work that led to your acceptance and your scholarship. Wake Forest is a fine college. Have you decided on your major?"

"No, ma'am, I can't decide between history and English. I love both subjects, but I'm sure of one thing: I want to be a teacher like you, Miss Thorne. Well ... not *exactly* like you."

Miss Thorne smiled and said, "I understand, Melissa. You will develop your own style of teaching, your own methods. I'm confident that you'll do well."

"Miss Thorne, may I ask you a personal question? You don't have to answer. It may be too personal, but this is the last day of school, and everyone knows you're retiring. You've been my English teacher for all four years, from freshman year through senior year. This morning, I realized that after today, I may never see you again. I've always wondered if … if you …."

"What is your question, Melissa?"

"Have you … This may be rude of me to ask—I know you've never been married—but … have you ever been … in love?" The last two words were blurted. Melissa's right hand flew up, covering her mouth. Her eyes widened. Her face reddened.

Miss Thorne did not answer. Instead, she opened the second drawer of her desk. She retrieved a framed photograph and handed it to Melissa. The young man in the black-and-white photograph was dressed in an Air Force uniform. He was fair-haired with squinting eyes of an indeterminate color. The young man smiled with the self-confidence of youth. Melissa's boyfriend smiled in that way.

"I loved him," said Miss Thorne. "He was very young when he died, only twenty-four."

"He's very handsome. Look here … he signed the picture. It says, 'To Grace, with all my love, Mark Evans.' His signature is so bold and strong."

"Yes, Mark had wonderful penmanship."

"What happened to him?"

"Mark was a test pilot, a very dangerous occupation. The official Air Force report said that one hour into his final flight, the test plane's controls malfunctioned. He crashed into the ocean near the Outer Banks. His body was never recovered."

"I'm sorry," whispered Melissa. "I'm so very sorry.

"No need to be sorry, my dear. He died a long time ago," said Miss Thorne. "Life goes on." She smiled and thumbed through the stack of essays.

"Melissa, here is your essay. You earned an A. I made some notes and comments on your composition. You may read them at your leisure."

In giving letter grades, Miss Thorne never said, "I gave you an A." She always said, "You *earned* an A." Of course, not all of her students earned As. However, she gave very few grades lower than C. Even the laziest of students would do their homework and write their essays for Miss Thorne. All the virtues and strengths that, when combined, made for a "good teacher" could be found in Miss Thorne.

Melissa returned the framed photograph to Miss Thorne's desk and accepted her graded essay. "Thank you, Miss Thorne. I don't know if I should ask you this ... Oh, I *know* I shouldn't, but I must ... Miss Thorne, did Mark Evans ask you to marry him?"

"Yes, he did."

"And did you accept his proposal, Miss Thorne?"

"Yes. Mark could be very persuasive. We were engaged to be married, but ... the accident, the crash. Everything ended so suddenly."

Miss Thorne studied Melissa's face. The teenager's lips trembled. *She's overcome with the tragic end of my romance,* the teacher thought. *Silly girl. She's only seventeen, and that's a silly age. She'll outgrow her silliness just as I did.*

When she was Melissa's age, Miss Thorne had been a silly girl, easily infatuated by a handsome boy and brokenhearted at the end of her several high school romances. Her students, old and young, would never have believed that Miss Thorne had ever been a teenager. They were more likely to believe she had been born middle-aged with a grammar book under her arm.

Should I tell Melissa my secret, she thought, longing to tell someone. *No, no, I mustn't. I mustn't tell her any more about Mark. I can't confide in her. I'm Melissa's teacher, not her friend.*

Miss Thorne would never tell Melissa about her first movie dates with Mark, about their long walks along dirt roads that paralleled the sunlit New River, about slow dancing to music coming from her Philco radio, about the good-night kisses which grew more passionate and culminated with the loss of her virginity in the backseat of Mark's Ford convertible.

Miss Thorne wanted to tell Melissa that Mark proposed after a picnic on Bluff Mountain. It was a colorful autumn day with blazing red and yellow trees burning through the valley below. She wanted to tell Melissa how she felt at that moment. She wanted to tell Melissa how happy and safe she felt in Mark's arms.

No! Not another word about Mark, she thought. *Besides, Melissa's too young. She couldn't possibly understand.*

"Miss Thorne, may I do something for you? I know! I'll erase the chalkboard. Is that all right?"

Miss Thorne nodded.

Melissa erased four neatly diagrammed sentences. She recalled when she was a freshman, and Miss Thorne had taught her freshman classes how to diagram sentences.

Melissa remembered mastering, at last, the placement of adverbs and prepositional phrases in the diagrams.

Melissa finished erasing the chalkboard and glanced down at Miss Thorne's open briefcase. Her mouth fell open. "Oh, Miss Thorne, is that a Ouija board? In your briefcase, is that a Ouija board?"

Miss Thorne closed her briefcase and snapped it shut. "No, child, it's a magazine with a *picture* of a Ouija board on the cover. Yesterday, I took the magazine away from one of my sophomore students. He was pretending to read from his textbook, but he was, in fact, looking through the magazine. Suffice it to say that it was not a proper magazine for a boy his age to be reading."

"Sophomore boys can be so immature," said Melissa, sounding much older than her seventeen years. "Well, I've finished erasing the chalkboard, and doesn't it look clean? Do you want me to dust your erasers? I can take them outside."

"No thank you, Melissa. Now you must run along. First period classes will begin shortly. Classes will be shortened on this last day. School will be dismissed at one o'clock. Goodbye, dear. You're in my third period class, so I'll see you then."

"Goodbye, Miss Thorne. I'll not tell anyone about your being in love, I promise. I'll not tell a soul about Mark Evans. It will be our secret. Some girls my age can't keep a secret, but I can."

"Yes, Melissa. It will be our secret. Goodbye."

The bell rang to begin the school day. The day passed in a blur of gangly blue-jean-clad freshmen boys, sophomore girls in knee-length skirts, short-sleeved junior boys with sunburned arms, and teary-eyed seniors, carrying yearbooks and dressed in their caps and gowns. Seniors were scheduled to practice for graduation at two o'clock.

Miss Thorne had made lesson plans for the abbreviated classes on this last day of school. Her freshmen would read and discuss "Old Christmas Morning," a Kentucky mountain ballad written by Roy Helton. *This poem is also a ghost story,* thought Miss Thorne. *My students should enjoy the mountain dialect and the surprise ending.* She remembered how Mark Evans had enjoyed ghost stories. His favorite writer was Edgar Allen Poe. He once read aloud to her "The Raven," emphasizing the word "nevermore."

"Nevermore." What a desolate, horrible word, Miss Thorne reflected.

Today, her sophomore English class would read the poem "Crystal Moment" by Robert P. Tristram Coffin. The junior class would read "A Red, Red Rose" written by Robert Burns. The night before, Miss Thorne had prepared discussion questions for each poem.

Miss Thorne's senior classes would read "Dreams" by the black poet, Langston Hughes. After discussing the short poem, her students would be given time to exchange and sign annuals. She knew many of her seniors would ask her to sign their yearbooks. She had decided she would sign all the books in this manner: "Hold fast to your dreams. With love, Miss Thorne."

Never before had Miss Thorne used the word "love" in signing student yearbooks. On this last day, the love Miss Thorne felt for her students was not of the maternal variety. Rather, it was closer to the affection an old general, retiring after years of service, might feel for his battle-tested troops.

The day passed with Miss Thorne feeling as if she were in a daze. Her classes filed in and out of her room. The bright, scrubbed faces of her students gleamed, almost blinding her. For the first time in many years, she felt tears in her eyes. Her students never noticed, or if they did, they said nothing.

At one o'clock, bells rang to dismiss the students. One by one or two by two, like ghosts in a movie, teenagers disappeared as they passed through her classroom door.

***

Outside her classroom, teachers lined up to say their goodbyes to Miss Thorne. The teachers did not crowd into her classroom but visited one by one. In the hall, they waited for their turn to speak to the retiring teacher. At the back of the line stood Clarence Beardsley, the school's principal. When his turn came, Mr. Beardsley entered Miss Thorne's classroom and said, "It was me."

"It was *I*, Clarence, but this is no time for formal English," laughed Miss Thorne, shifting in her chair.

"I was the one who, so many years ago, put the onion on your desk. I removed the apple that was there and replaced it with an onion. The other boys dared me to do it. I was in your freshman English class at Jefferson High School. I was in your sixth period class, the last class of the school day. Do you remember?

"I remember. Many years have passed since then. Clarence, you were a ... a lively freshman boy, full of mischief."

"It was only today that I gathered enough courage to admit my prank," said Mr. Beardsley.

"Yes, I remember the incident well because that spring I had begun working on my master's degree at Appalachian. In addition to summer school, I was taking late-afternoon, weekend, and night classes. My professor had asked his students to bring a souvenir, a memento from their classrooms. I surveyed my classroom: the chalk, the erasers, several pens, the English textbooks, literature books, perhaps my roll book. They would not do. I decided to take your onion, Clarence. It provoked quite a discussion. Later, I took it home and made a soup of it."

"I'm glad it proved useful."

"The next year, your sophomore year, I found five or six thumbtacks strategically placed on my chair. I discovered them before I sat down, thank goodness. I suspected you, Clarence, of the deed."

"It was ... it was I," confessed Principal Beardsley. "After ten years as your principal, I have never gathered the courage to tell you about those thumbtacks until now. I must've been a slow learner, for it was not until my junior and senior years that your lessons began to sink in. You convinced me of the value of a good education. You encouraged me to read anything I could get my hands on—comic books, newspapers, magazines, and novels. I still remember the day you brought a stack of Classics Illustrated comic books to class. I read the comic book version of *The Adventures of Huckleberry Finn*, and the next day, I went to the library and checked out the novel. I've read Twain's novel many times since then. In your English classroom, you taught me and the others to *think* rather than to memorize. After reading *Silas Marner*, I earned an A on my essay about foreshadowing in the novel. I still have that essay. I keep it in my desk drawer at home. I owe you a tremendous debt of gratitude, Miss Thorne."

"You owe me nothing, Clarence. It was your own inner strength, your curiosity, and your intellect that made you a fine student, both in high school and in college. As a principal, you have involved teachers in your decision-making process. That is so rare. Working with you has been my pleasure. Perhaps I owe *you* a debt of gratitude."

"Miss Thorne, could I prevail upon you to stay with us one more year? It will be difficult to ... to replace ...."

"No, Mister Beardsley, my decision is final. You'll understand if you remain in the profession for forty years."

"Very well, I understand. Will you attend our graduation ceremonies tonight?"

"Yes."

"Goodbye, Miss Thorne. Thanks for ... for everything."

After the principal's departure, Miss Thorne looked around her classroom. She would work at the school tomorrow along with the other staff, but there would be no students at the high school. The day would be spent taking an inventory of supplies, counting textbooks, and reviewing end-of-the-year test scores with the principal.

She picked up her briefcase, closed and locked her classroom door, and walked down the long hall leading to the exit doors. Outside, she used her right hand to shield her eyes from the bright sunshine. She walked briskly toward her car. She wondered if *he* would be waiting there. Sometimes he was; sometimes he wasn't.

She reached her old, black Chevrolet, opened the heavy door, got inside, and slammed the door shut. Miss Thorne placed her briefcase in the passenger seat. She inserted the ignition key and turned it. The car's engine came to life. She let the engine idle. She did not look in the backseat for fear that he would not be there. A chill that began in the back of the car crept to the front seat. That was good. Her breath was visible as it spread in a frosty mist. She looked in the rearview mirror.

He *was* there. He was reclining in the Chevrolet's backseat. He rose to a sitting position.

He was dazzling in his Air Force uniform. Medals decorated his blue jacket. His trousers were pressed, and his polished shoes gleamed. His pilot's cap, worn at a jaunty angle, hid most of his golden hair. His face and hands were tanned, and his blue eyes glittered.

"Hello, Mark. Thank you for waiting for me, darling. It must've been terribly dull for you, just sitting here in the car."

"Nonsense, I enjoyed watching the students come and go. Some arrived in buses, some arrived in cars. Some left in cars, some left in buses. Besides, I couldn't miss your last day of school. "

"Did they see you? Did the students see you?"

"Gracie, you're the only one who can see me. You know that."

"Yes, I know, but sometimes I forget."

He leaned forward from the backseat and touched her on the shoulder. Miss Thorne had gotten used to his cold touch. Still, she shivered. She smiled and turned to face him.

"What is it, Mark?"

"Darling Grace, would you do me a favor? Could we stop by Weaver Cemetery on the way home? My old friend Frank Thompson will be there. He's just arrived. Automobile accident, you know. He'll have questions about his transition. I can help him. I'd like to see Frank and a few others."

"Oh, Mark, it's so boring for me at the cemetery. I can see only you and can barely hear the others. Their voices are so deep and raspy. Can't we just go home and conjure with the board? You know that I must go to the graduation ceremonies tonight, and we will have so little time together. Must you go to the cemetery?"

"I won't be long, Gracie. Frank will need help to … to adjust. I'll speak with him. Then we'll go home. I'll read you a story—'The Masque of the Red Death' by Poe. After that, we can play our game using the spirit board. There will be a full moon tonight. Remember, you brought my spirit to you on such a night. And I'm so glad you summoned me. As you have learned, my dear, conjuring is always best with a full moon."

"All right, then. We'll stop at the cemetery, Mark, but only for fifteen minutes. Then we'll go home and play with the Ouija board."

On the steering wheel, Miss Thorne's hands trembled with excitement. Mark's cold hand reached forward and caressed her gray hair. Her eyes flashed, and she wet her lips with her tongue.

She and Mark loved to conjure up the dead using the Ouija board.

www.ingramcontent.com/pod-product-compliance
Lightning Source LLC
Chambersburg PA
CBHW030113260626
47156CB00008B/2640